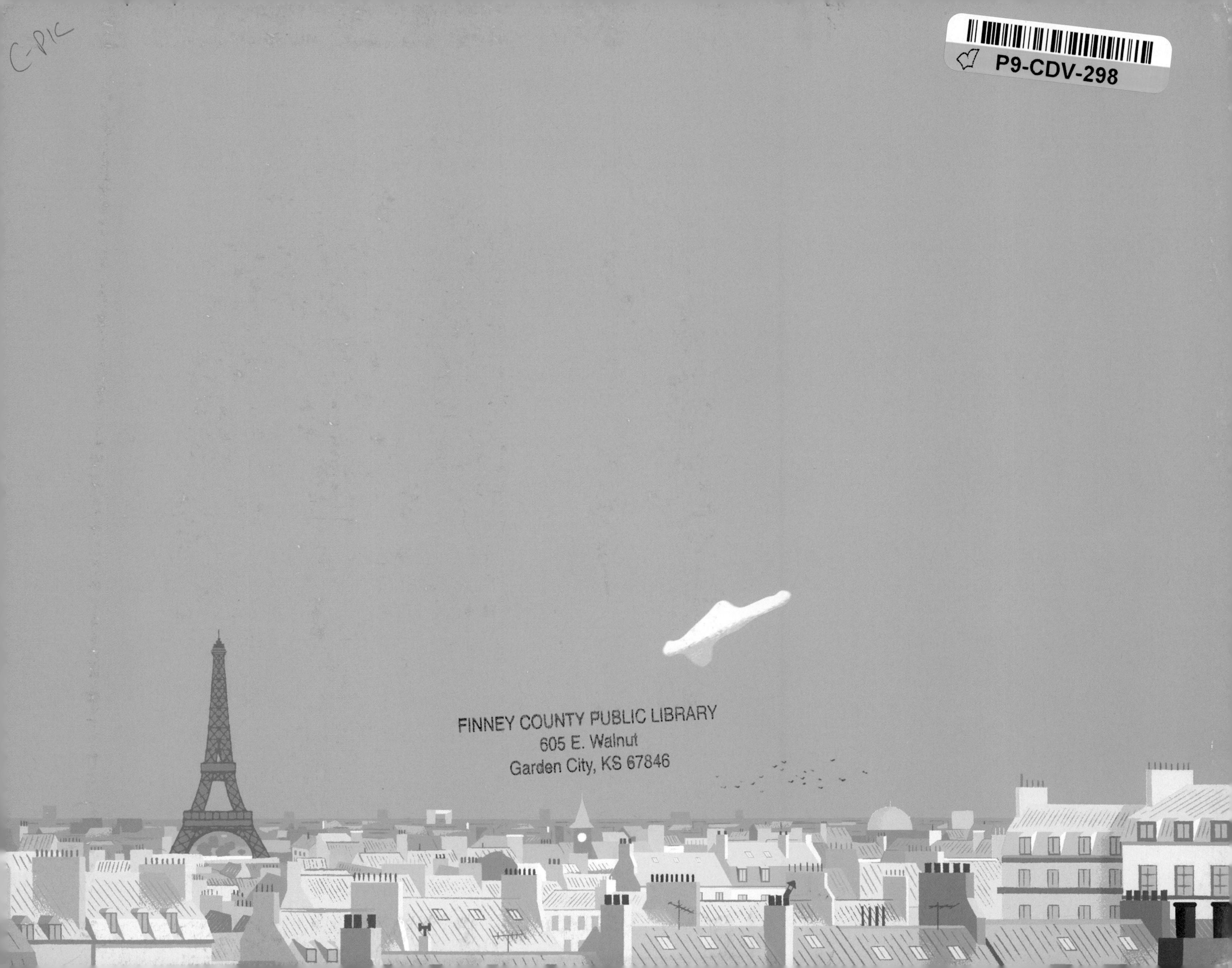

MY SINCERE THANKS GO TO JACQUES TATI, IN SPITE OF HIMSELF,
AND PIERRE ÉTAIX, MACHA MAKEÏEFF, JÉRÔME DESCHAMPS,
PHILIPPE GIGOT, AND "LES FILMS DE MON ONCLE".

ALSO PUBLISHED BY DAVID MERVEILLE,
LE JACQUOT DE MONSIEUR HULOT, 2005.

English translation copyright © 2013 by NorthSouth Books Inc., New York 10016.
First published in France under the title *Hello Monsieur Hulot*.
Hello Monsieur Hulot (text and illustrations) copyright © 2010 by Rouergue, France.

First published in the United States, Great Britain, Canada, Australia, and New Zealand in 2013
by NorthSouth Books, Inc., an imprint of NordSüd Verlag AG, CH-8005 Zürich, Switzerland.

Distributed in the United States by NorthSouth Books Inc., New York 10016.
Library of Congress Cataloging-in-Publication Data is available.
ISBN: 978-0-7358-4135-2 (trade edition)
Printed in China by Toppan Leefung Packaging and Printing (Dongguan) Co., Ltd., Dongguan, P.R.C., December 2013.
3 5 7 9 · 10 8 6 4 2
www.northsouth.com

www.merveille.be/david
www.tativille.com

Published with the participation of National Center of the Book.

NORTHSOUTH

PRESENTS

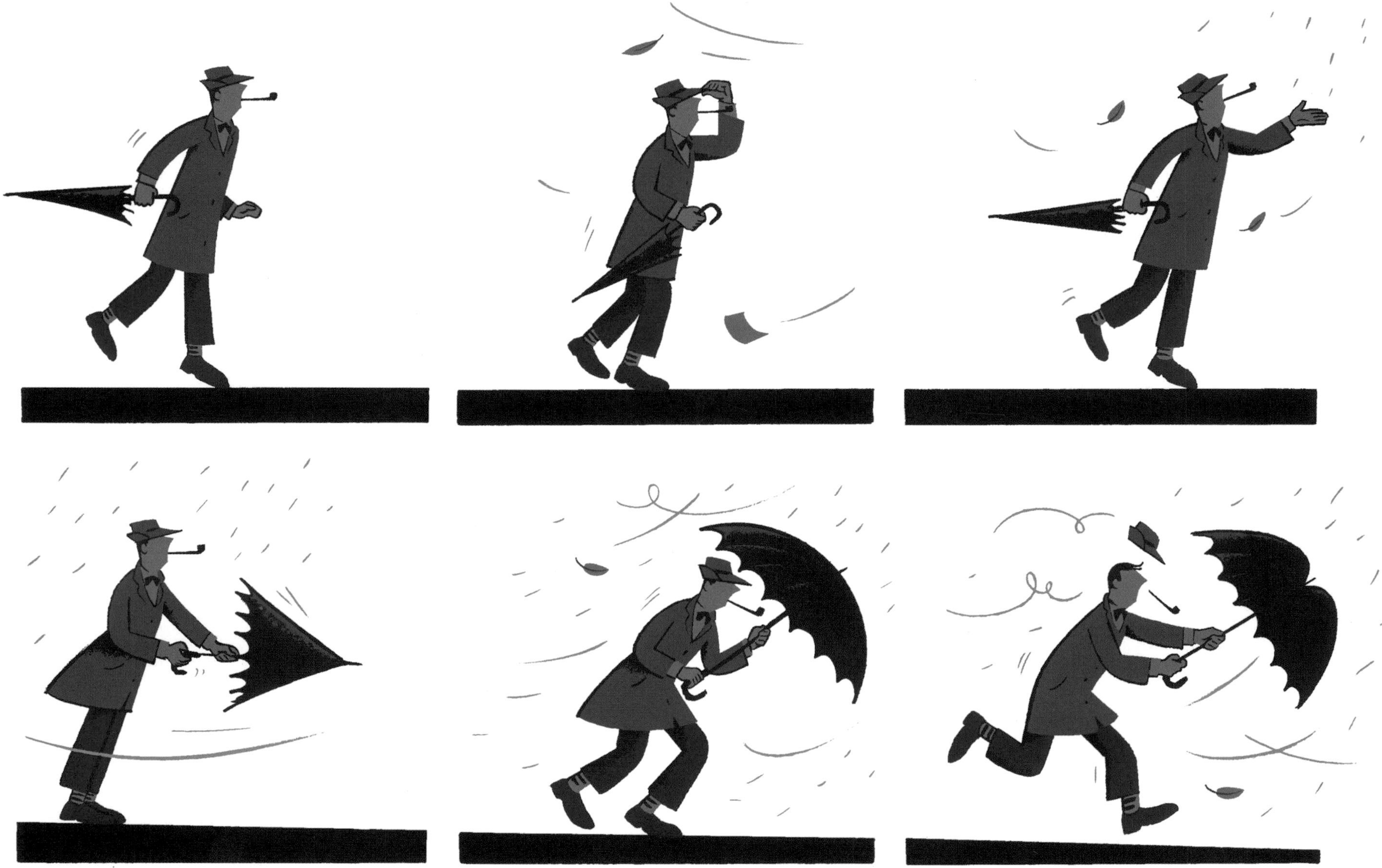

HELLO, MR. HULOT

DAVID MERVEILLE ACCORDING TO JACQUES TATI

North South

THE HEART OF PARIS

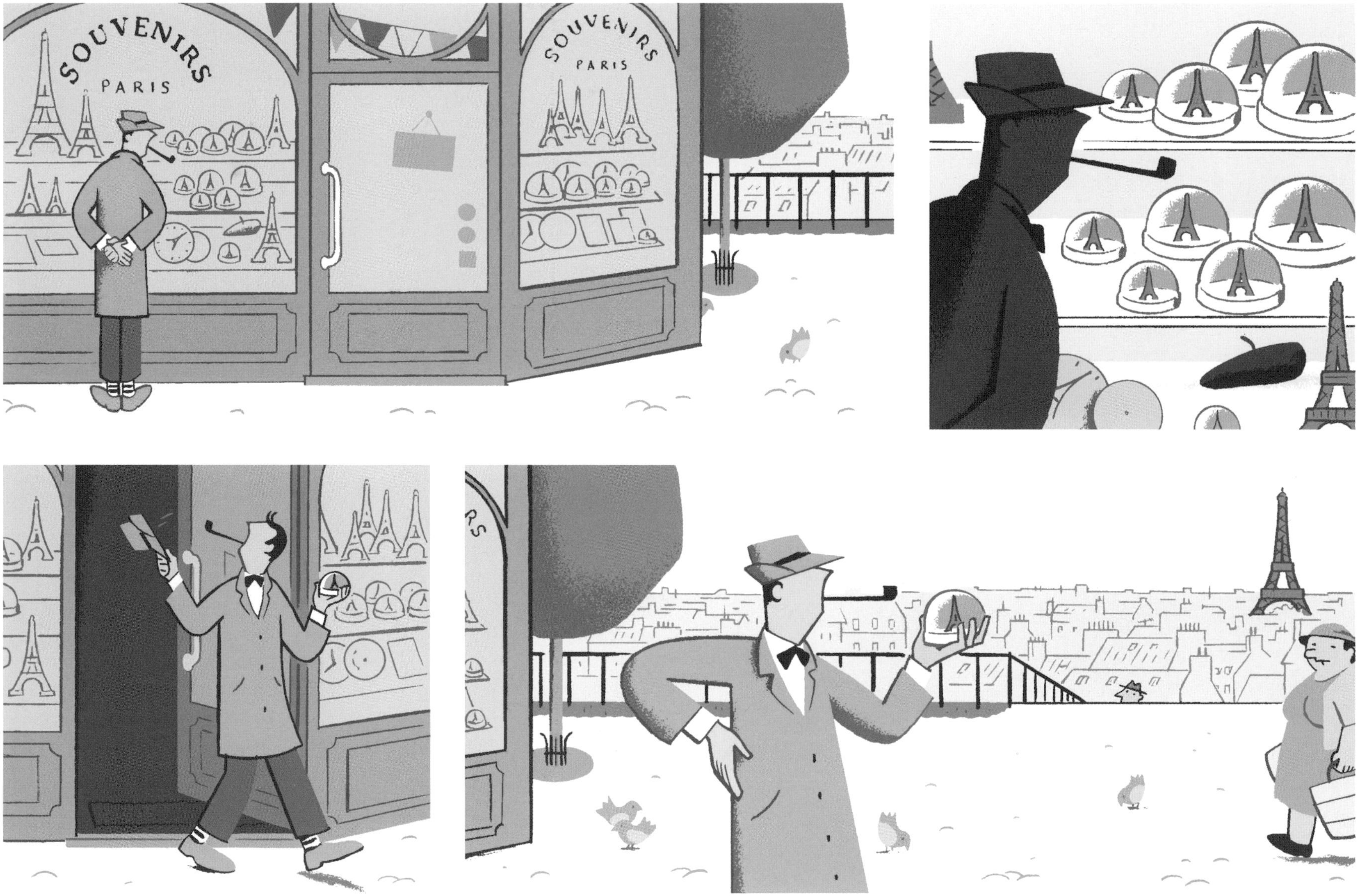
SOUVENIRS
PARIS
SOUVENIRS
PARIS

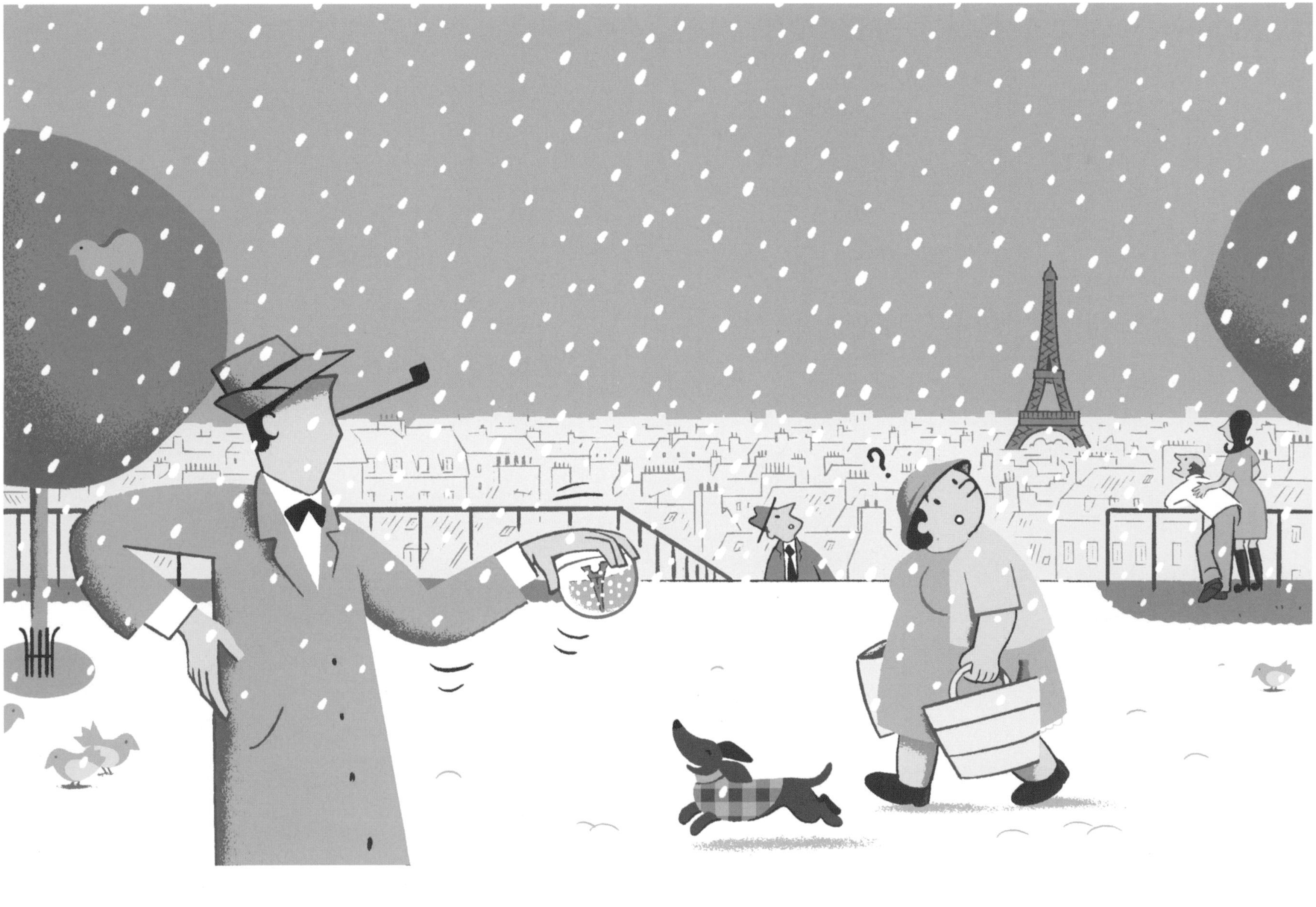

THE MOON WALK

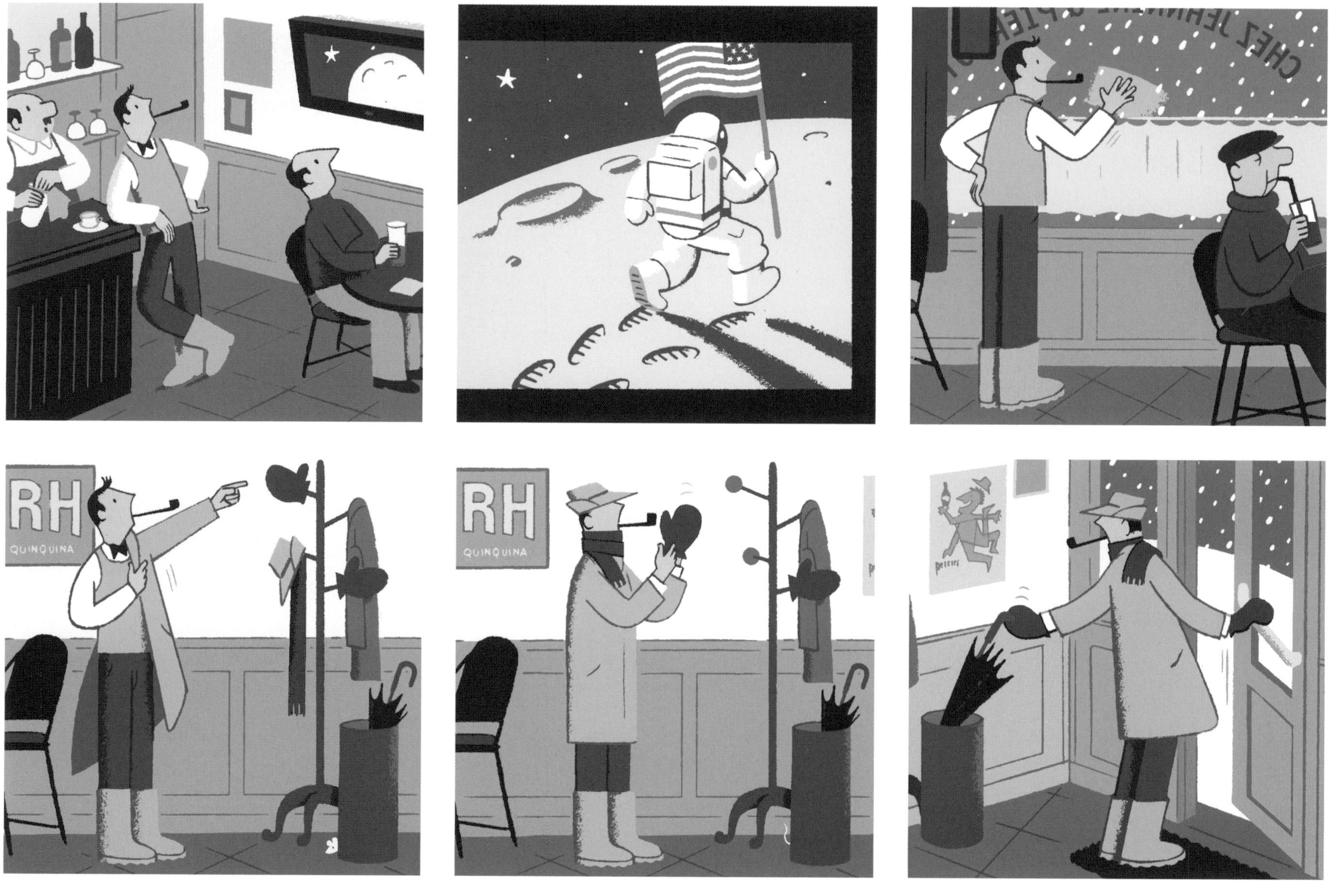
RH
QUINQUINA
RH
QUINQUINA

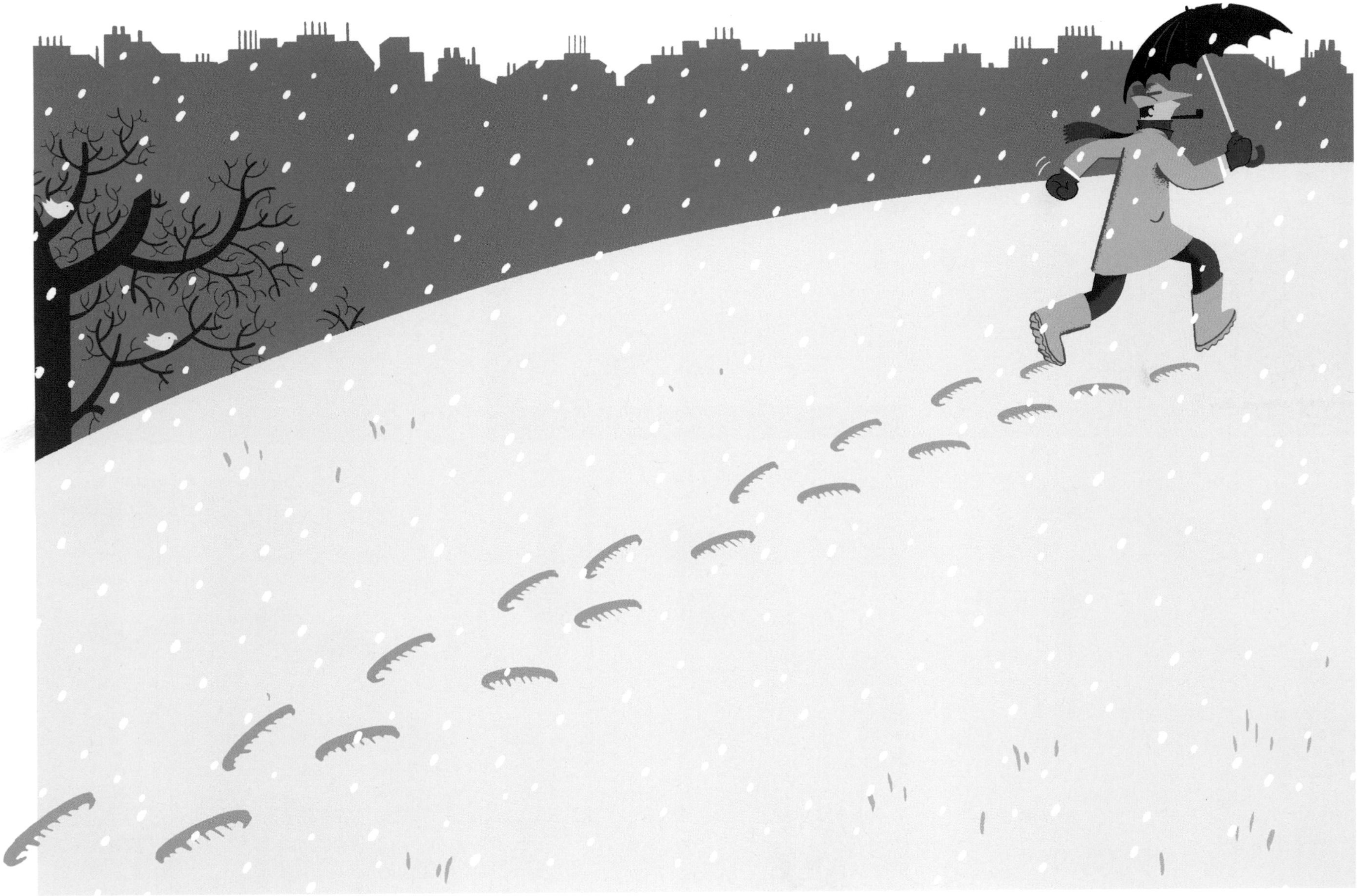

THE SNOWBALL EFFECT

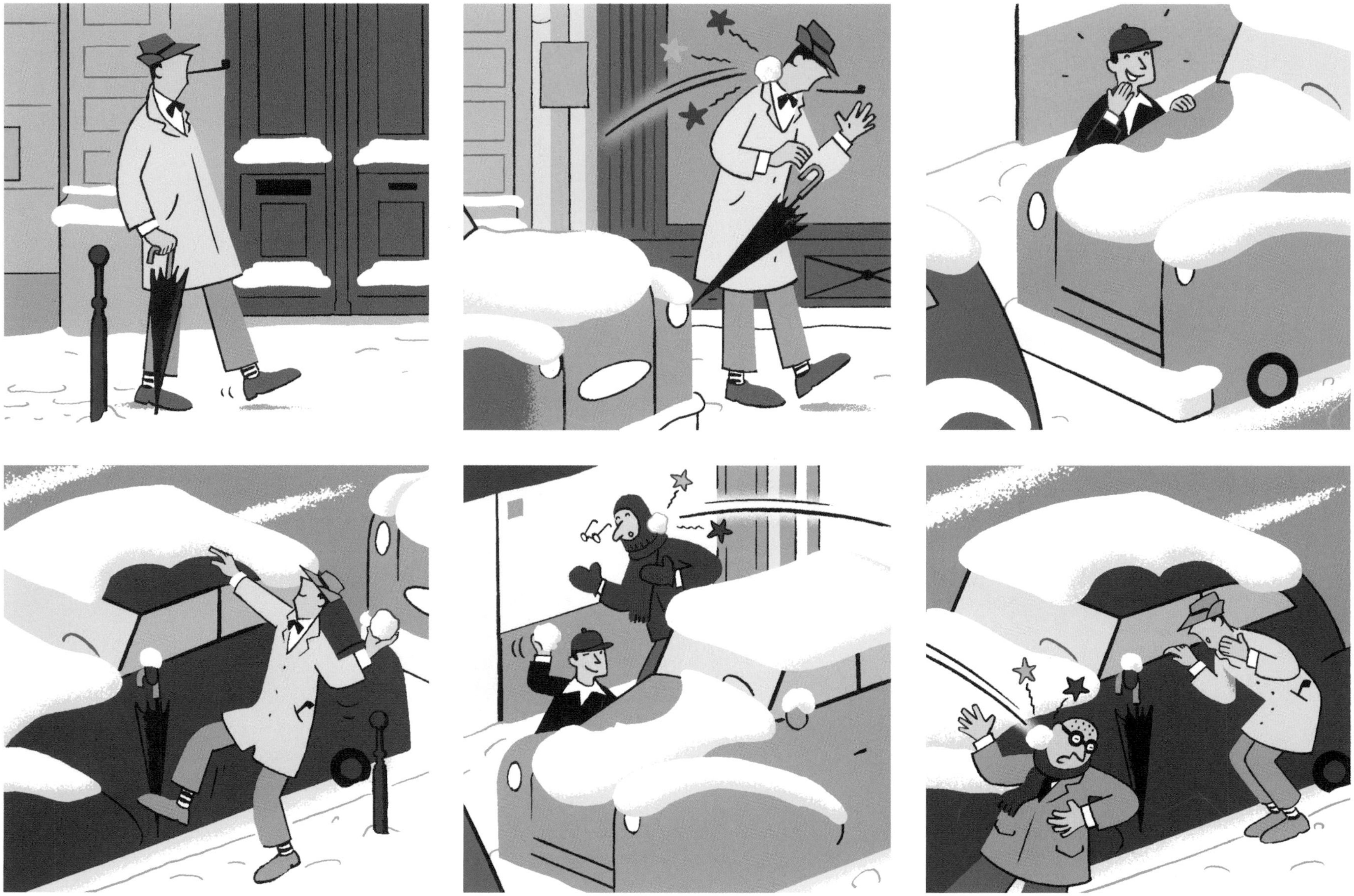

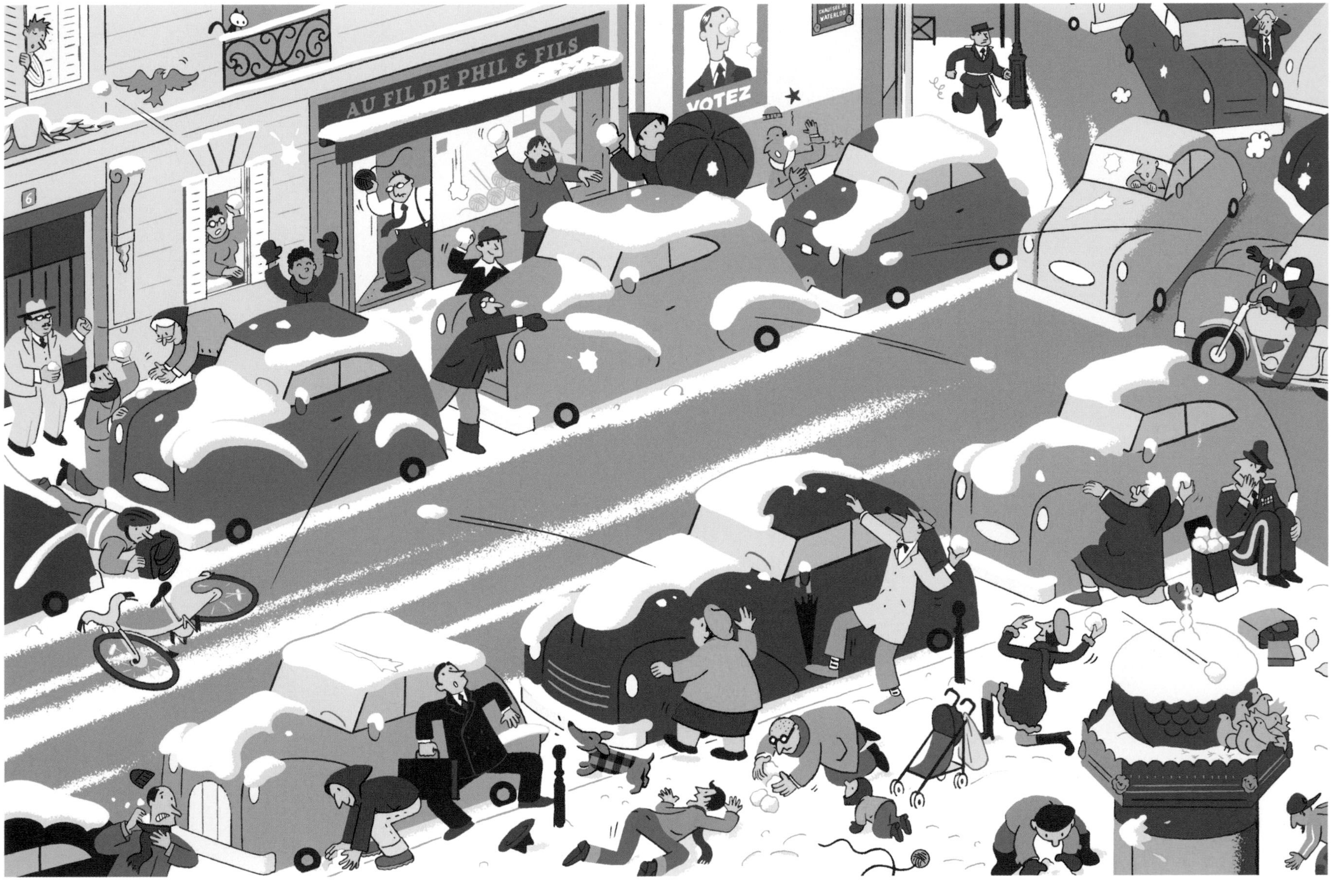
AU FIL DE PHIL & FILS
VOTEZ
CHAUSSEE DE
WATERLOO
6

GLOBE TROTTER

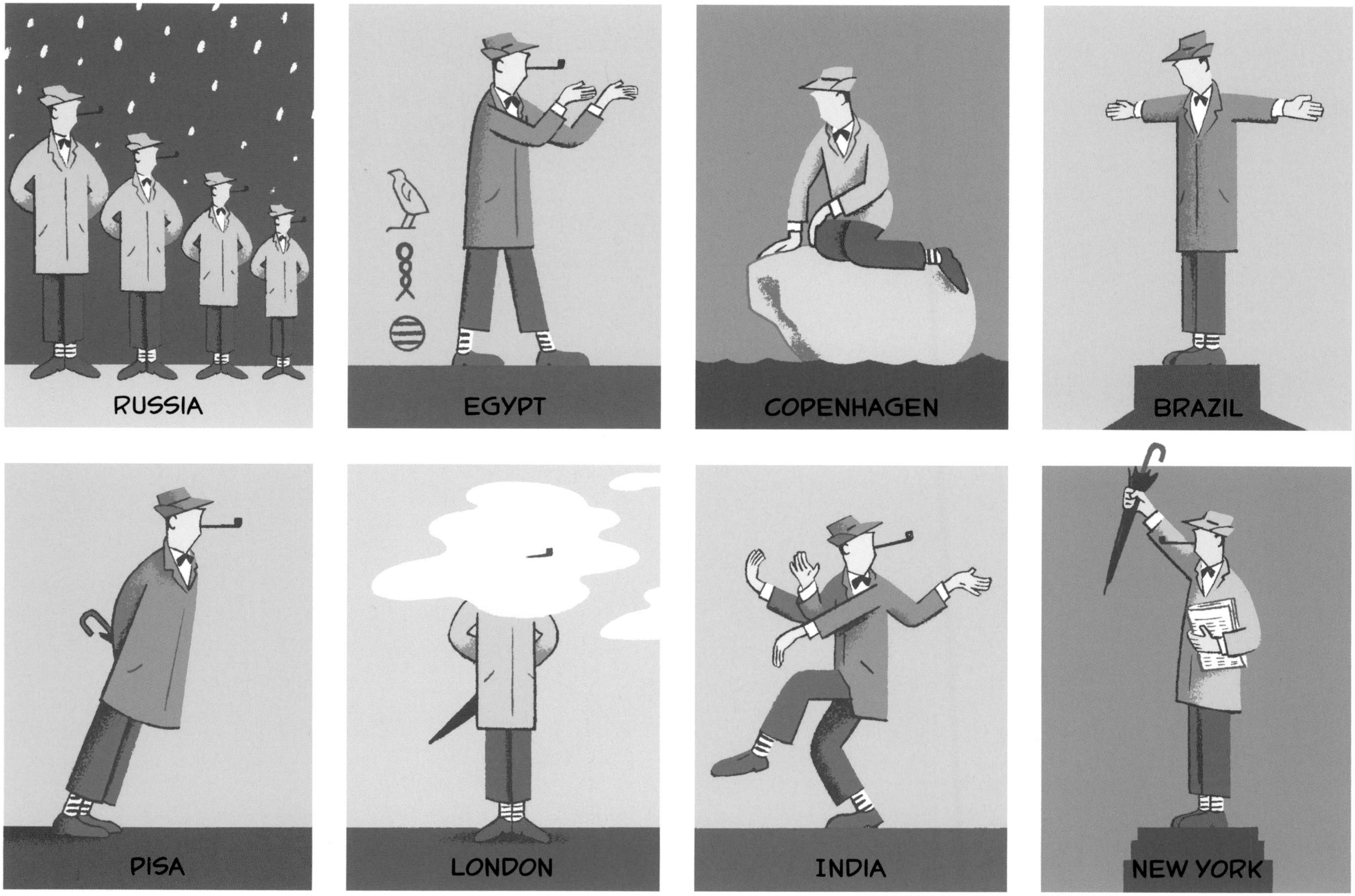
RUSSIA
EGYPT
COPENHAGEN
BRAZIL
PISA
LONDON
INDIA
NEW YORK

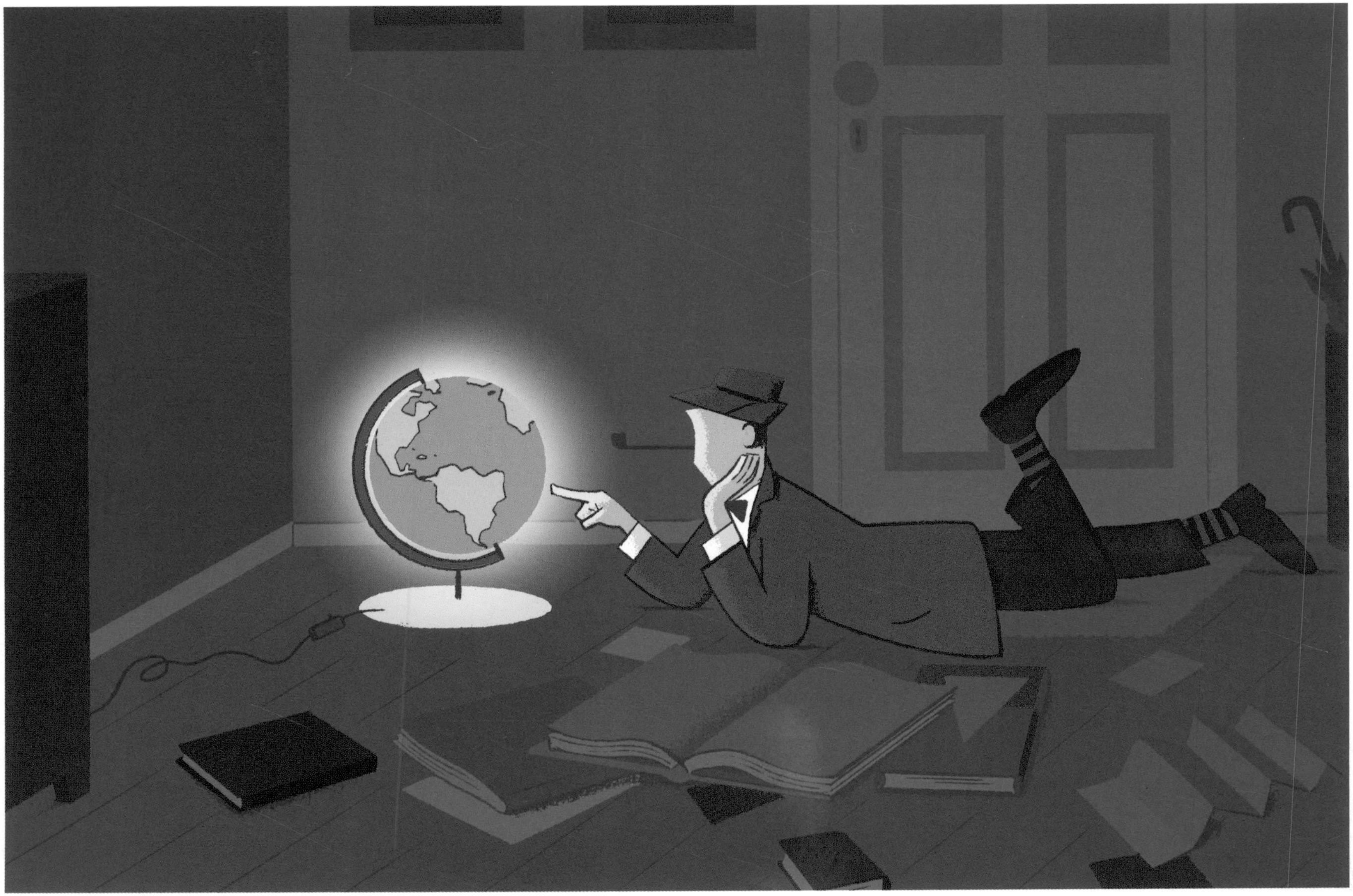

HULOT THE PLUMBER

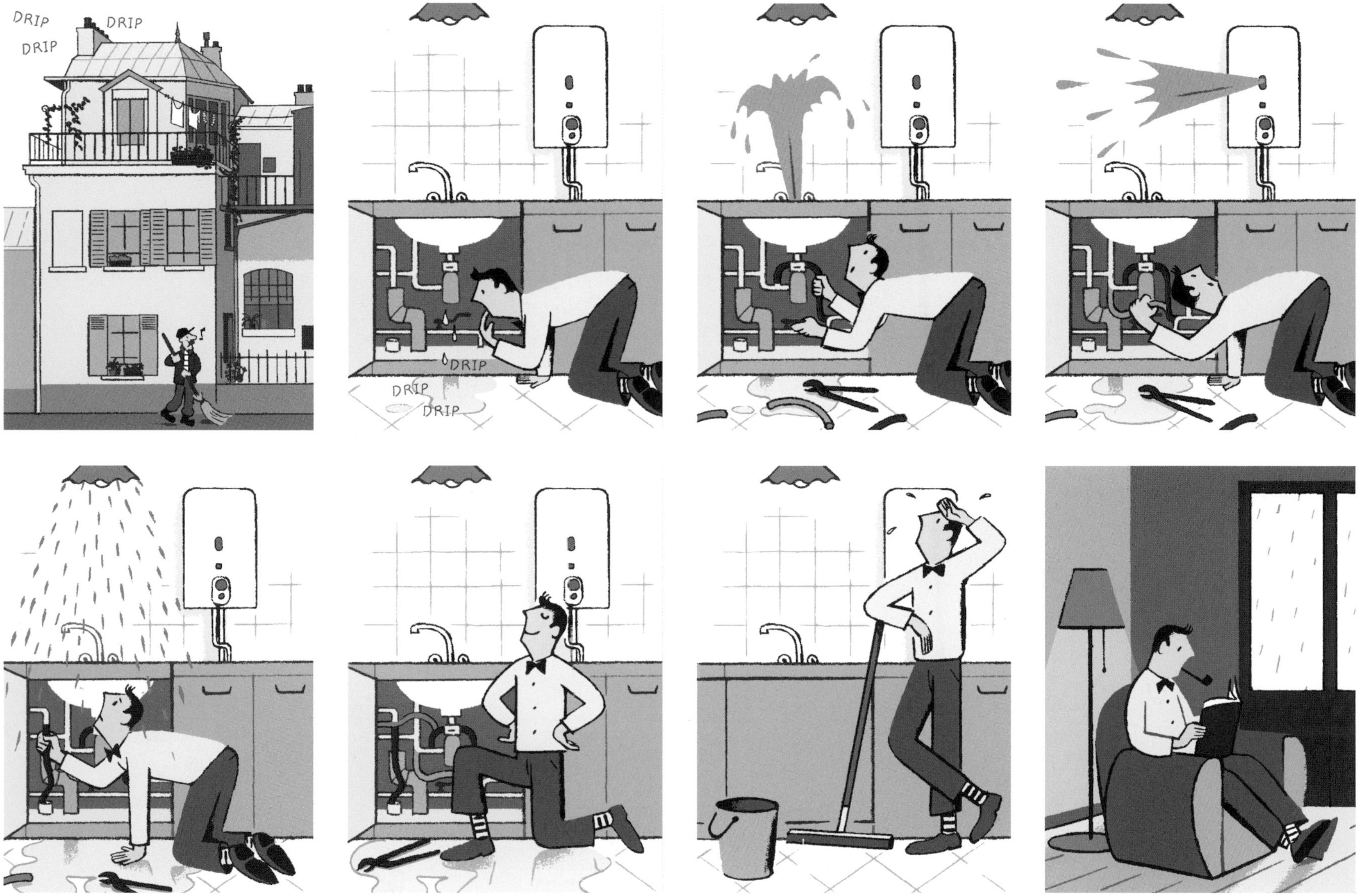
DRIP
DRIP
DRIP
DRIP
DRIP
DRIP

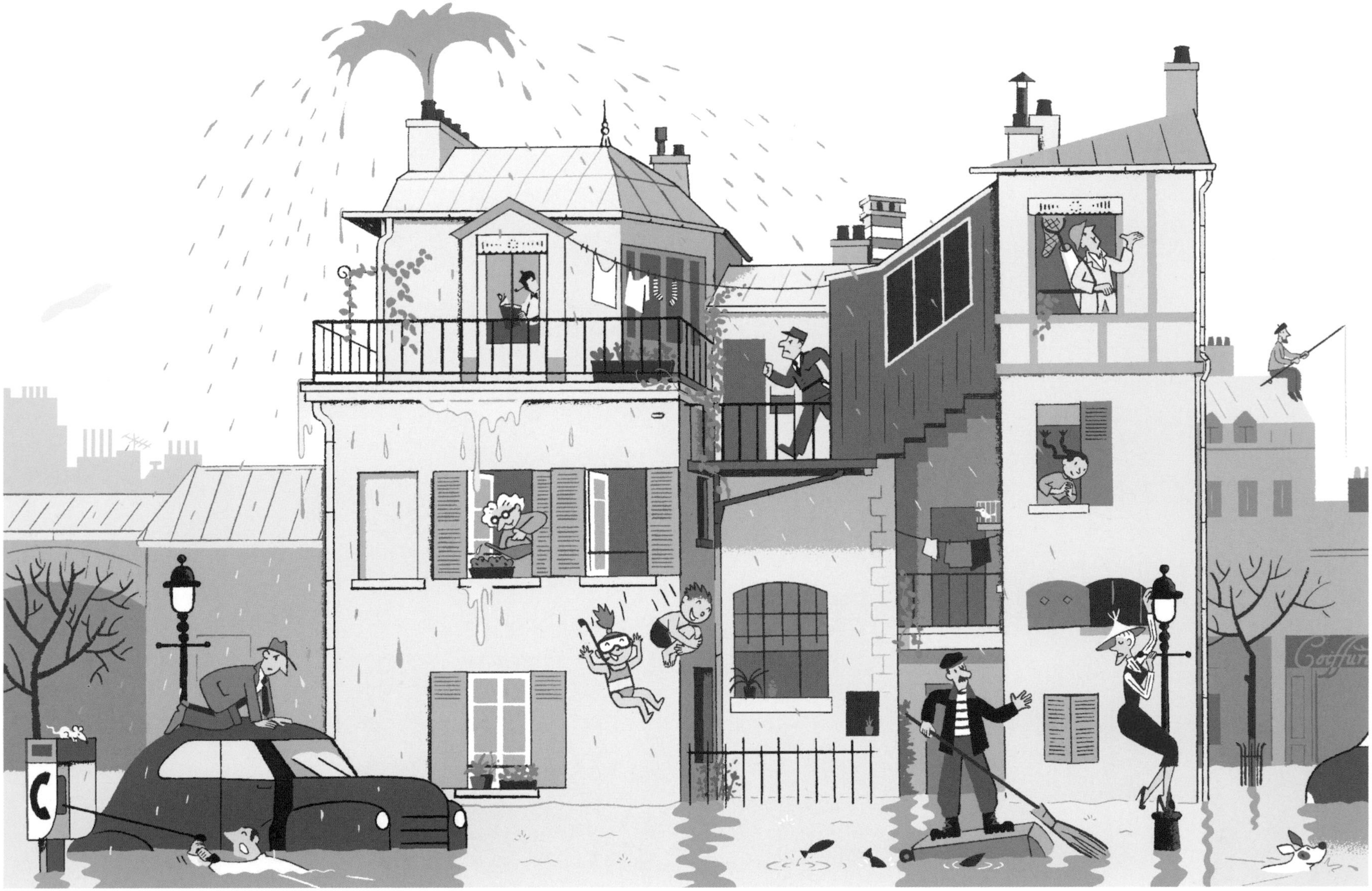

FRENCH RIVIERA

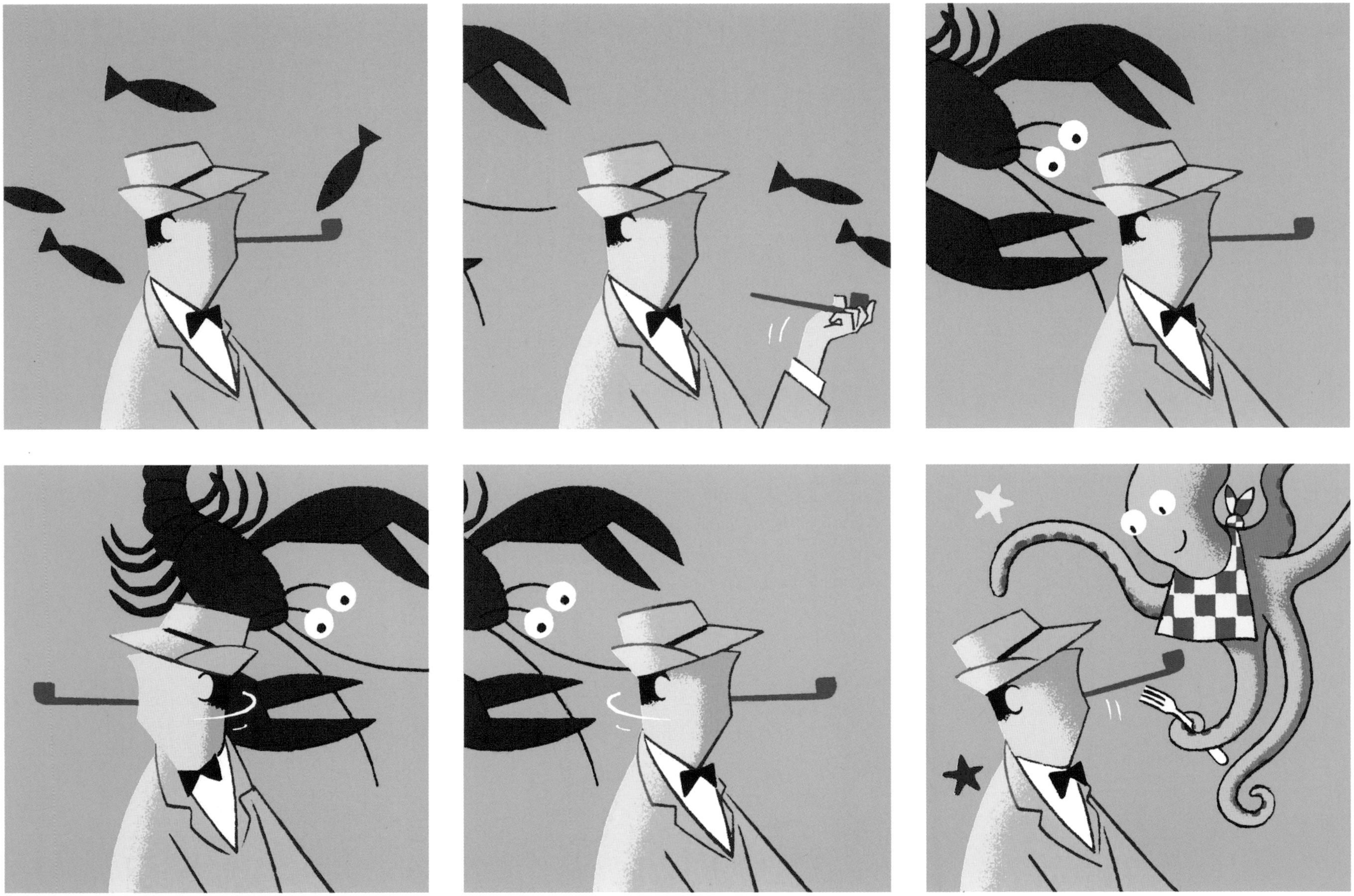

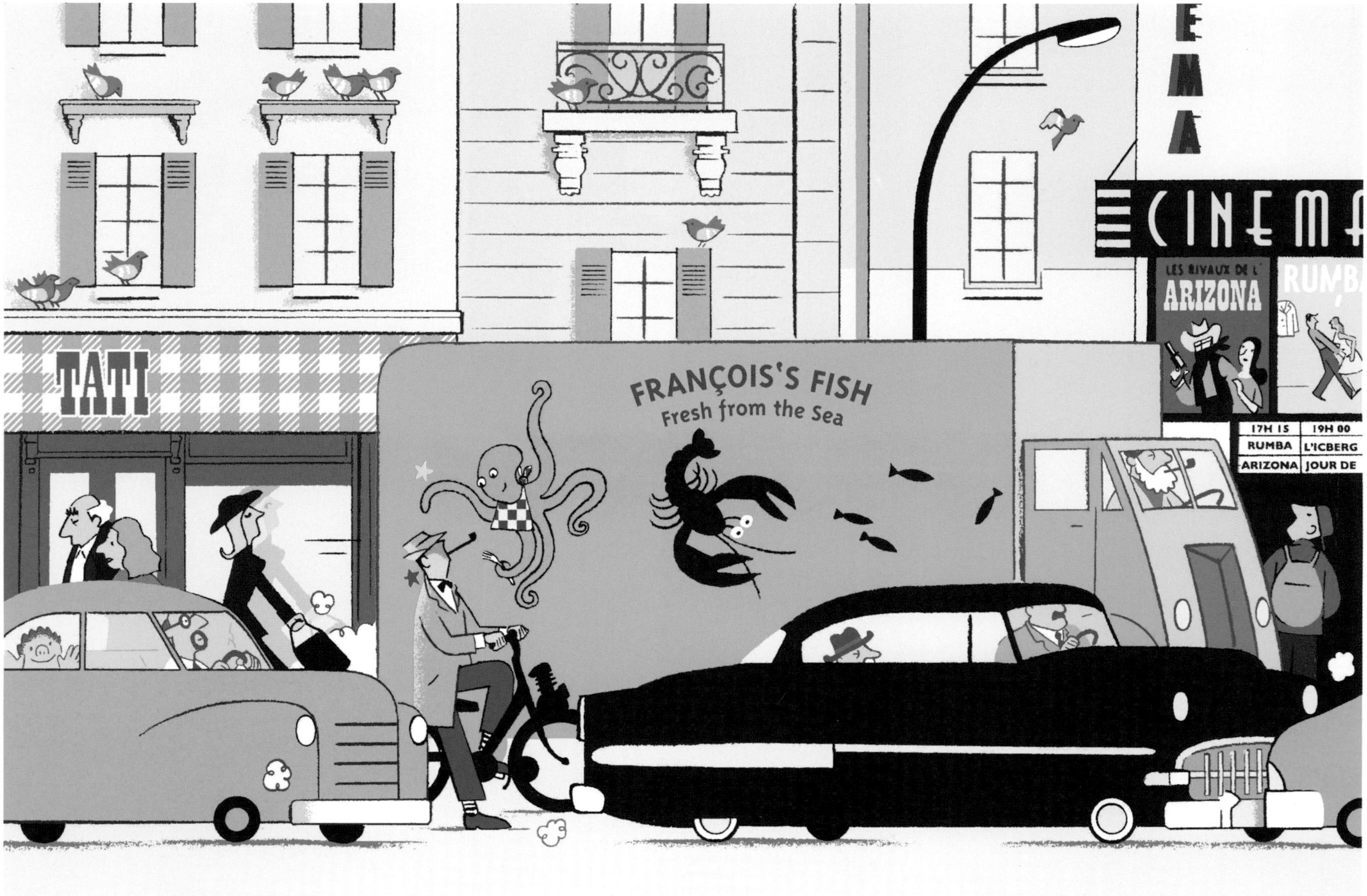
EMA
CINEMA
LES RIVAUX DE L'
ARIZONA
RUMBA
17H 15
19H 00
RUMBA
L'ICBERG
ARIZONA
JOUR DE
TATI
FRANÇOIS'S FISH
Fresh from the Sea

HULOT THE HERO

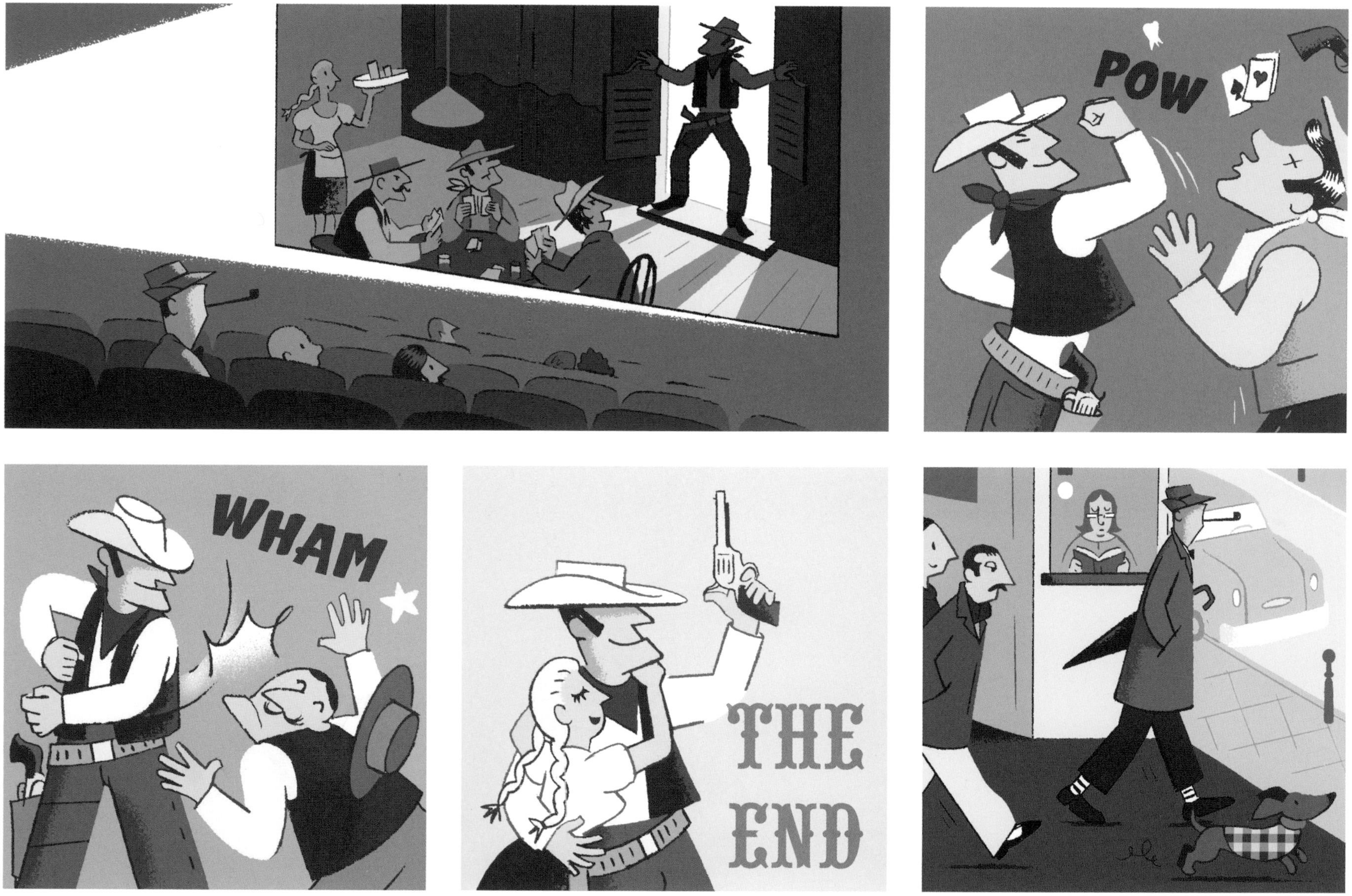
POW
WHAM
THE END

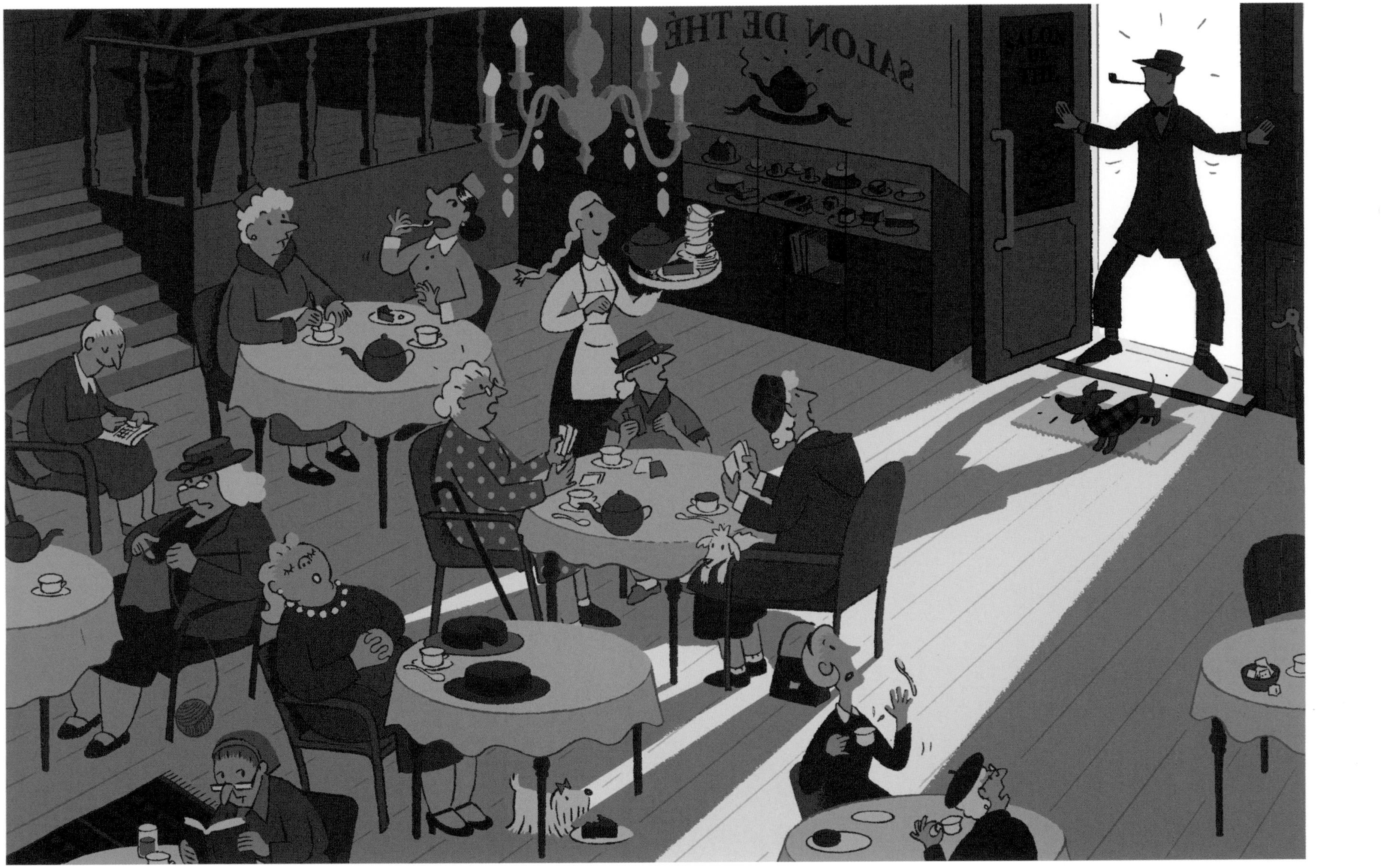
SALON DE THÉ

THE UMBRELLA CORNER

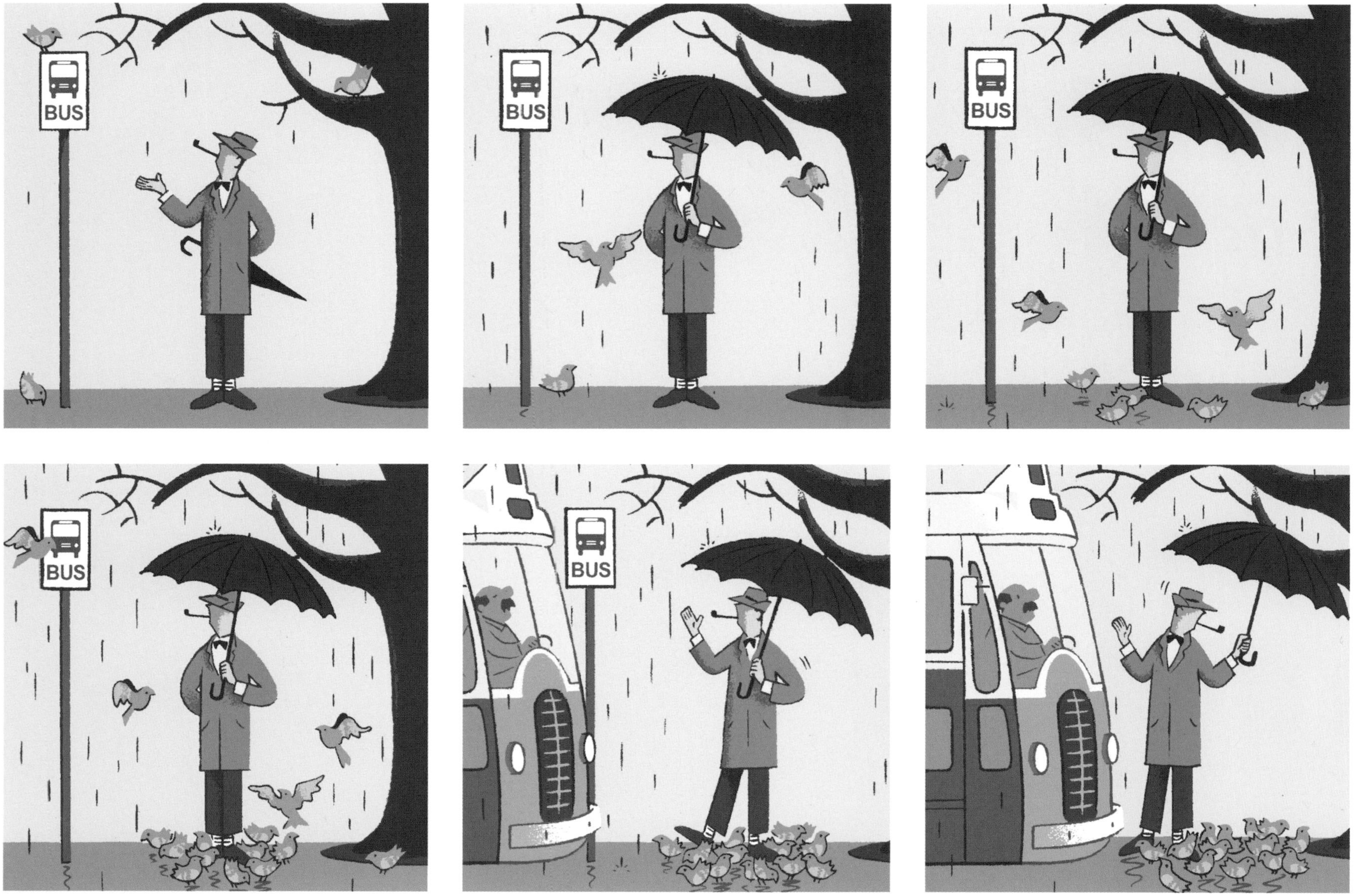
BUS
BUS
BUS
BUS
BUS

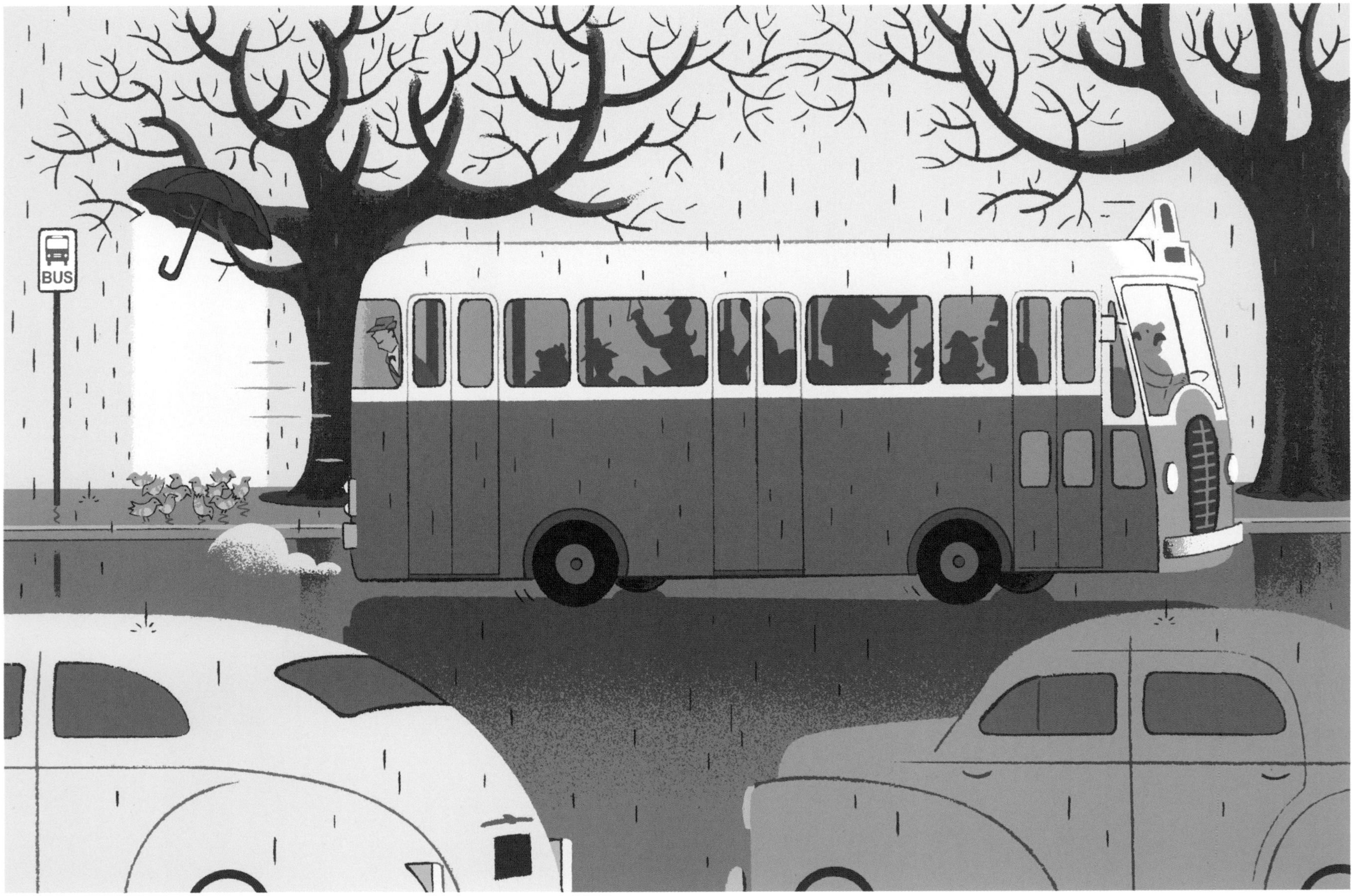
BUS

PIPES ALLOWED

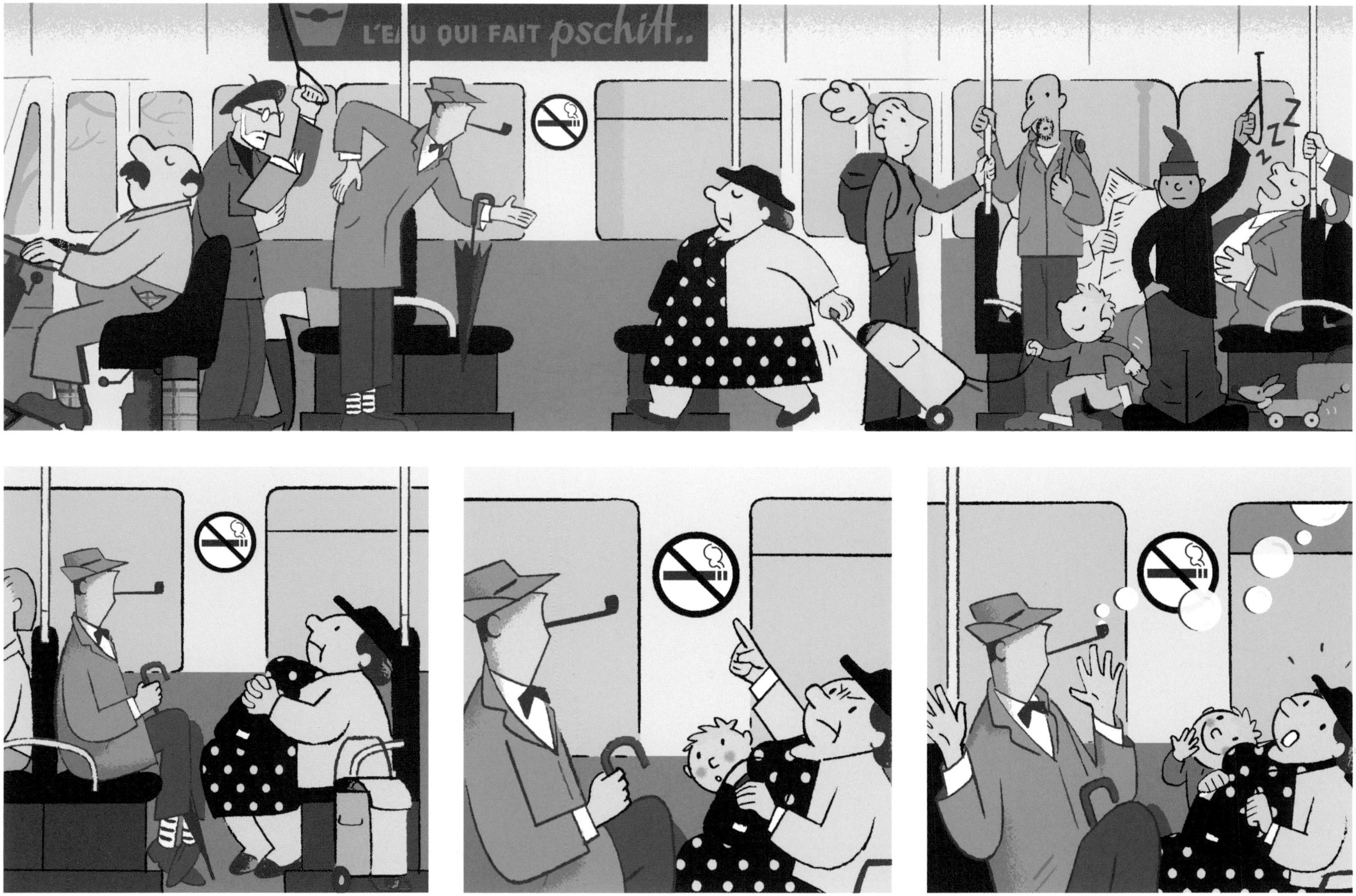
L'E U QUI FAIT pschitt..
Z Z Z

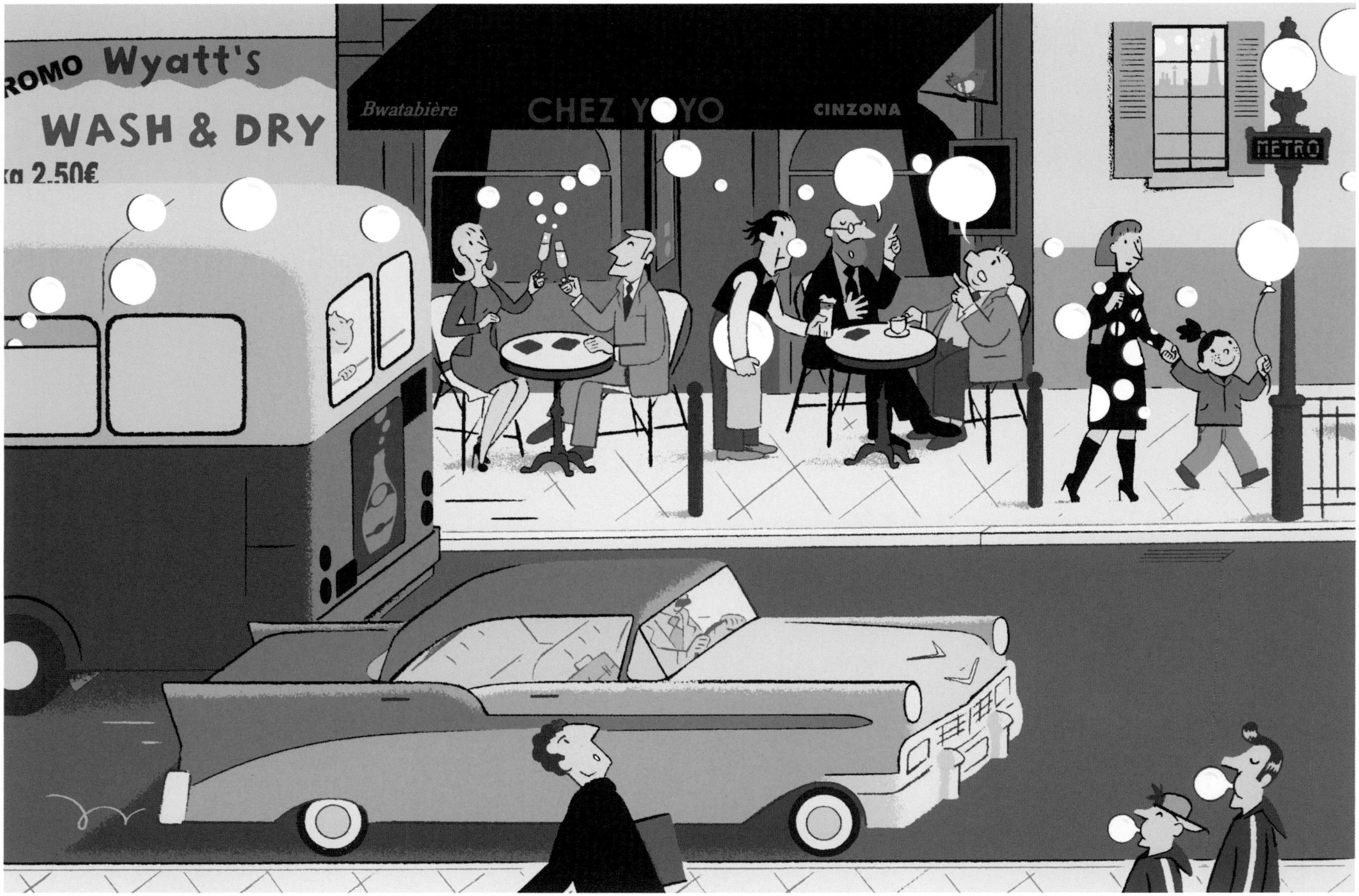
ROMO Wyatt's
WASH & DRY
ka 2.50€
Bwatabière
CHEZ YOYO
CINZONA
METRO

CHAMELEON

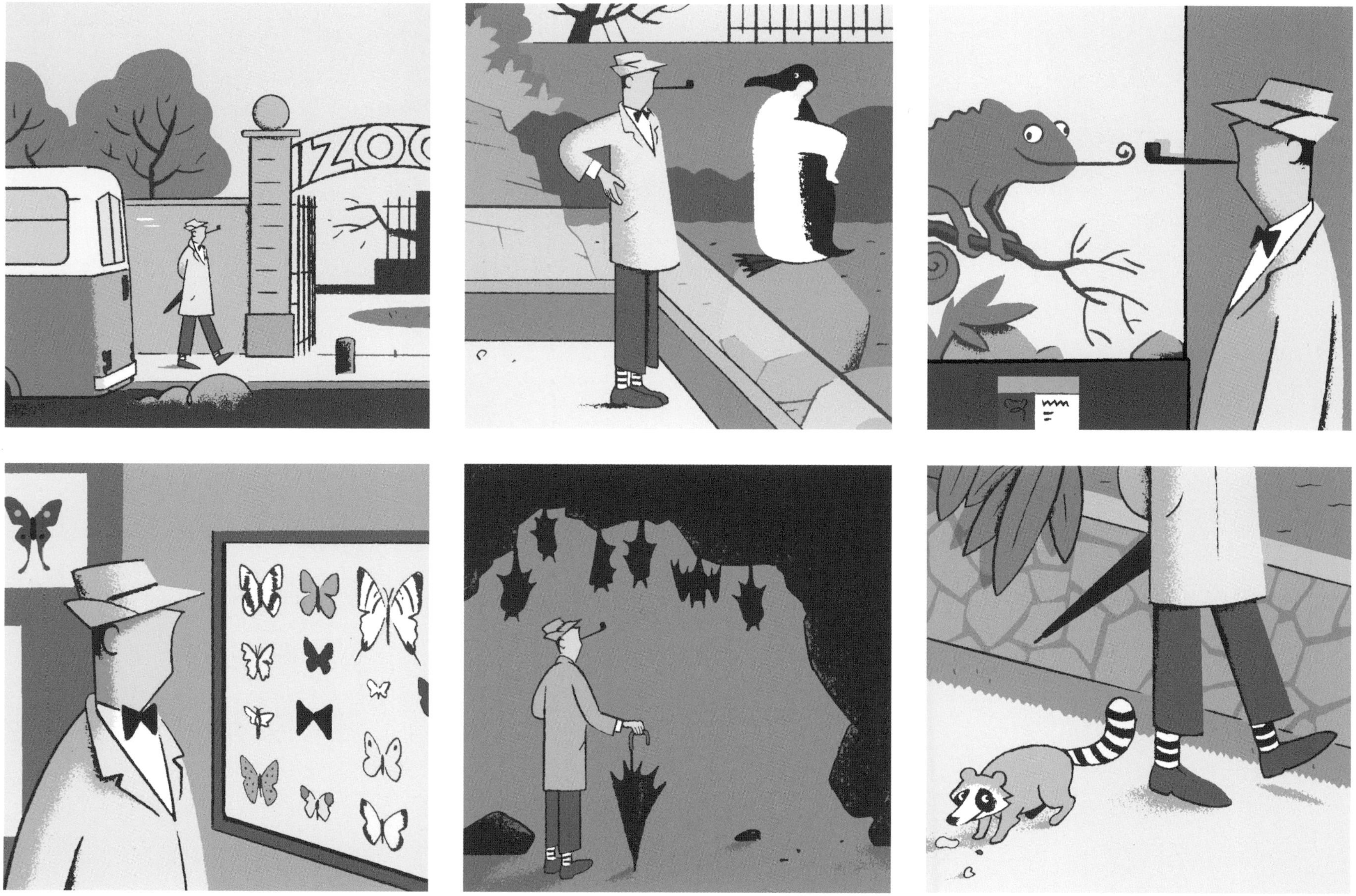

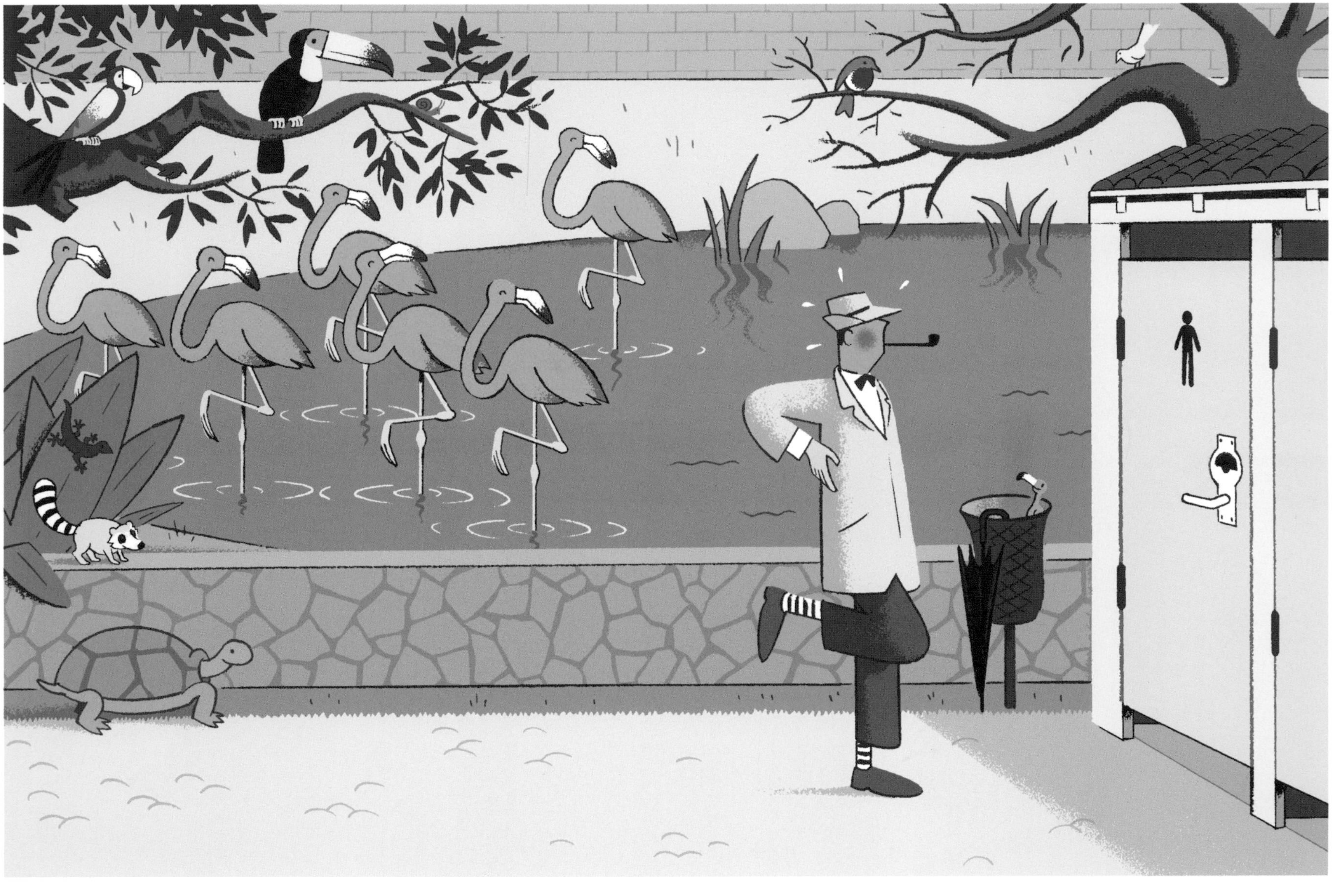

URBAN SYMPHONY

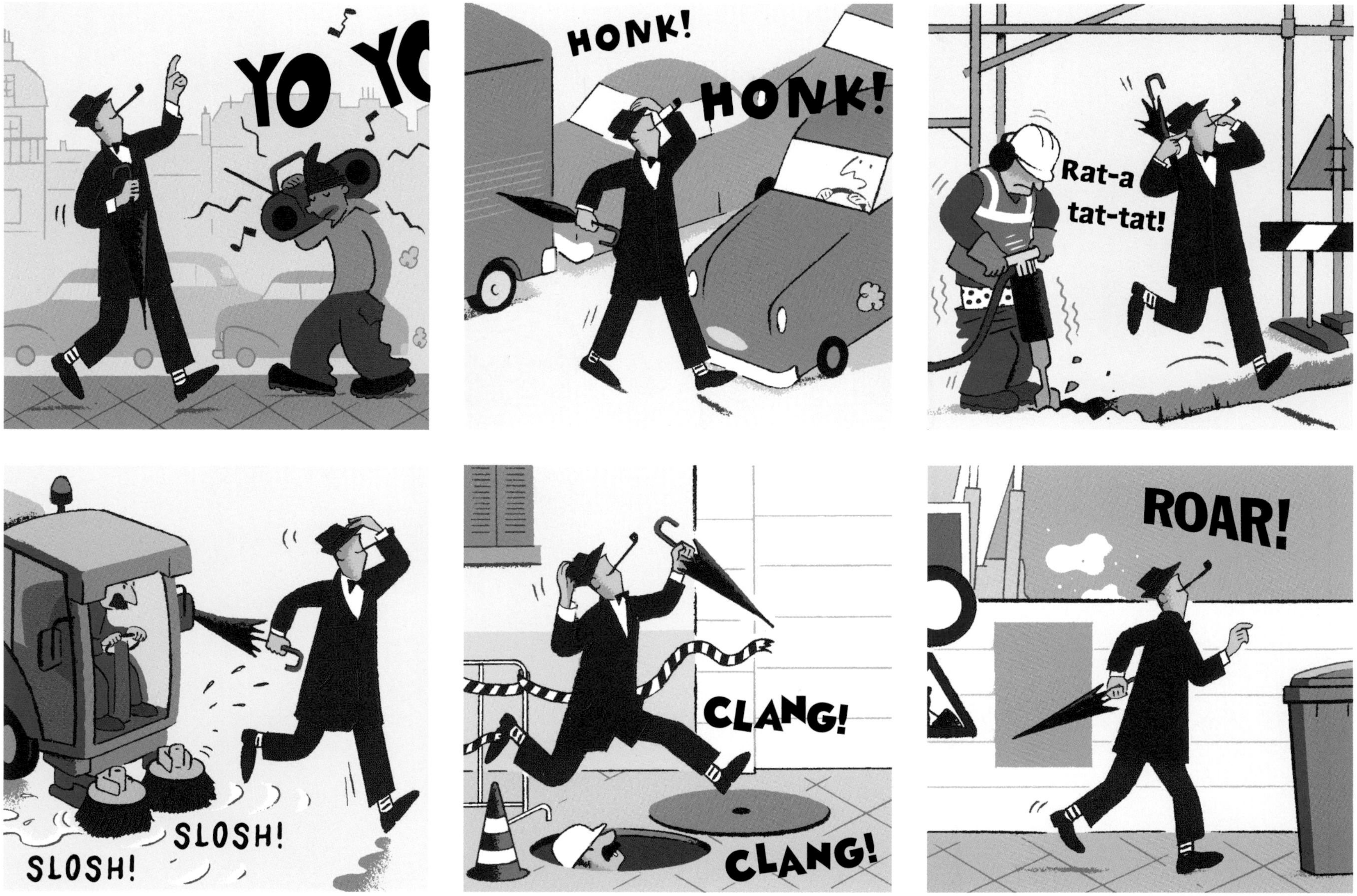
YO YO
HONK!
HONK!
Rat-a tat-tat!
SLOSH!
SLOSH!
CLANG!
CLANG!
ROAR!

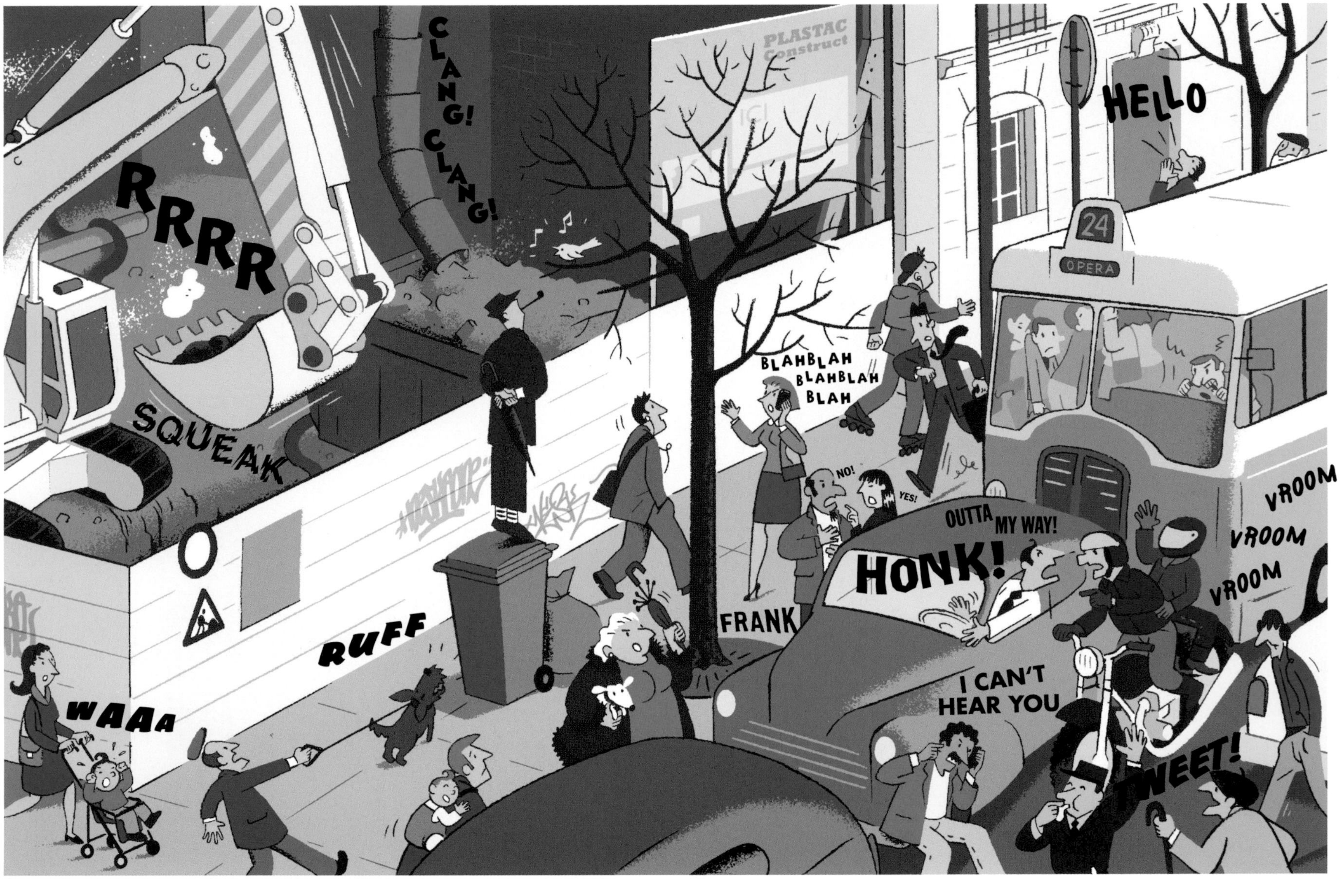
PLASTAC Construct
RRRRR
CLANG! CLANG!
SQUEAK
HELLO
24
OPERA
BLAHBLAH BLAHBLAH BLAH
NO!
YES!
OUTTA MY WAY!
HONK!
VROOM
VROOM
VROOM
FRANK
RUFF
WAAAA
I CAN'T HEAR YOU
TWEET!

A CHILD'S GAME

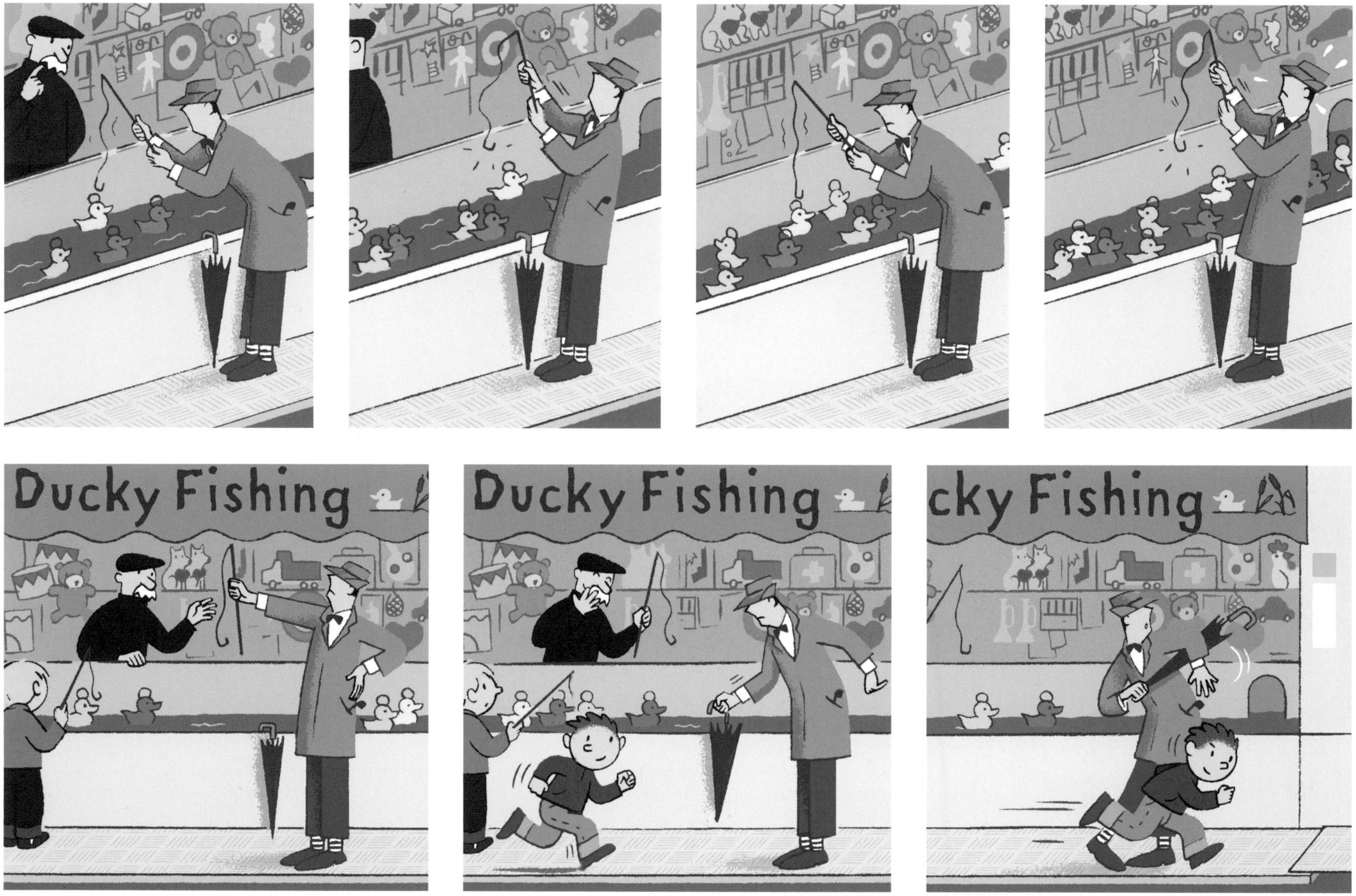

Ducky Fishing
Ducky Fishing
cky Fishing

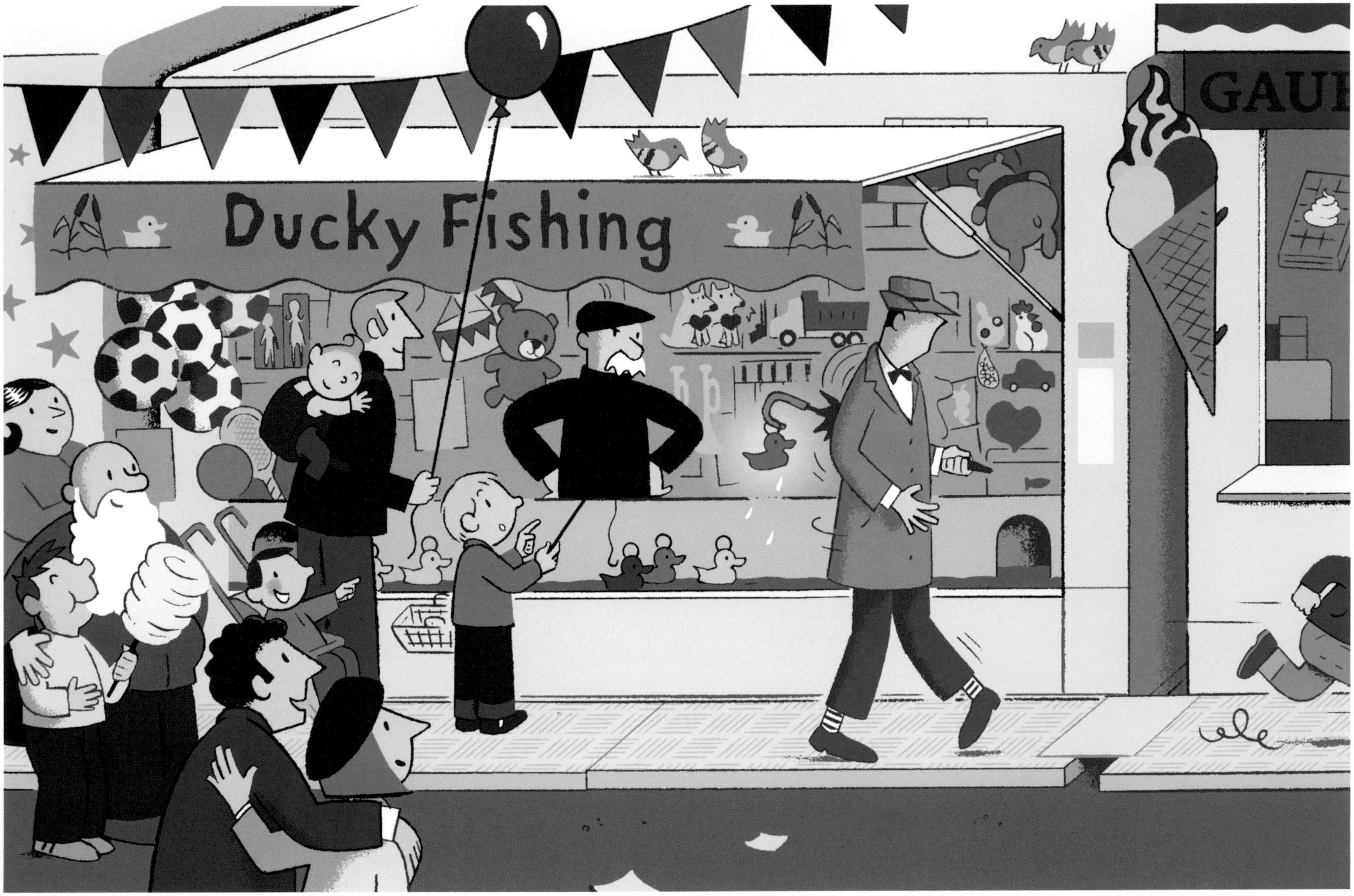
Ducky Fishing
GAU

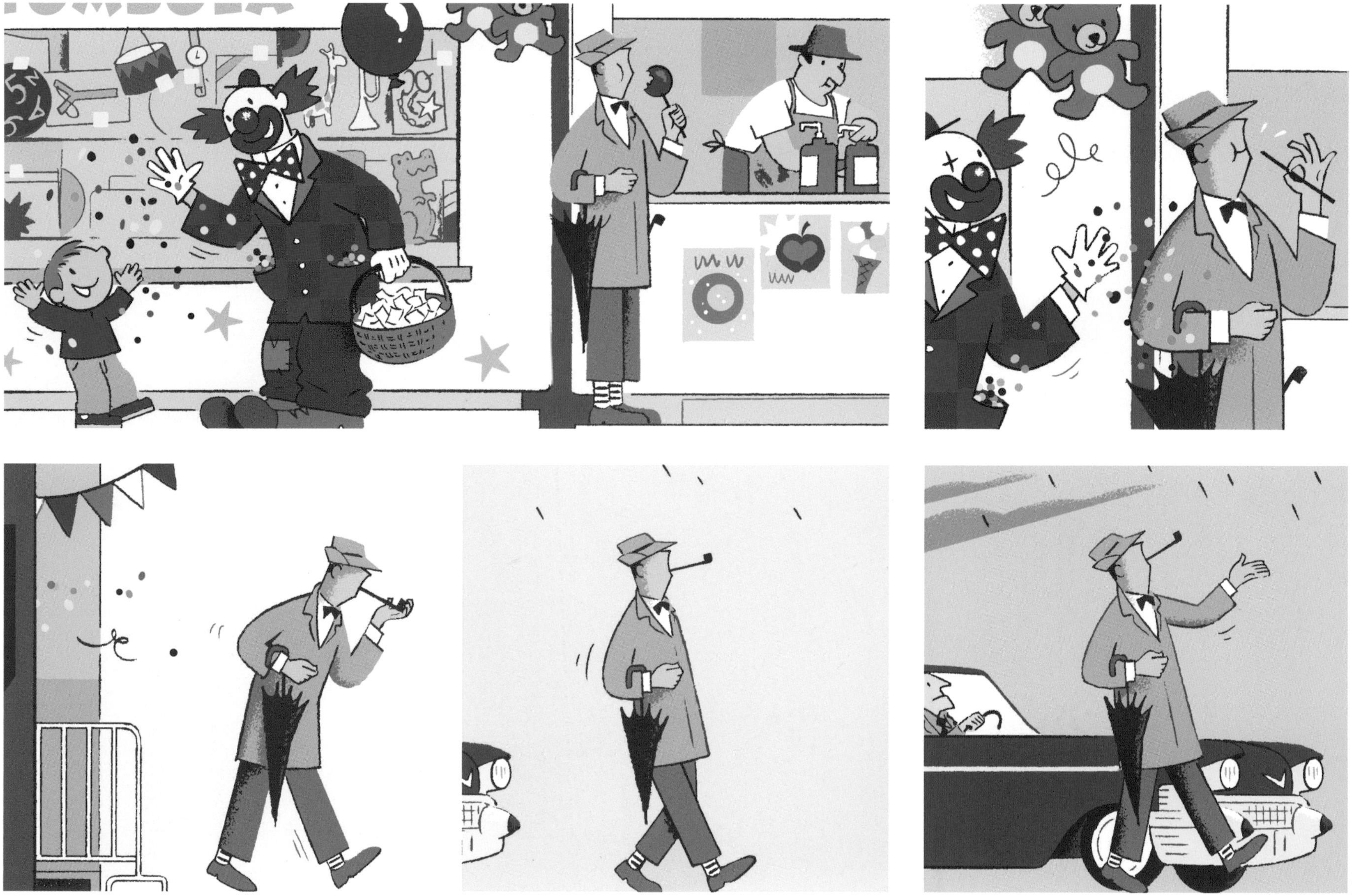

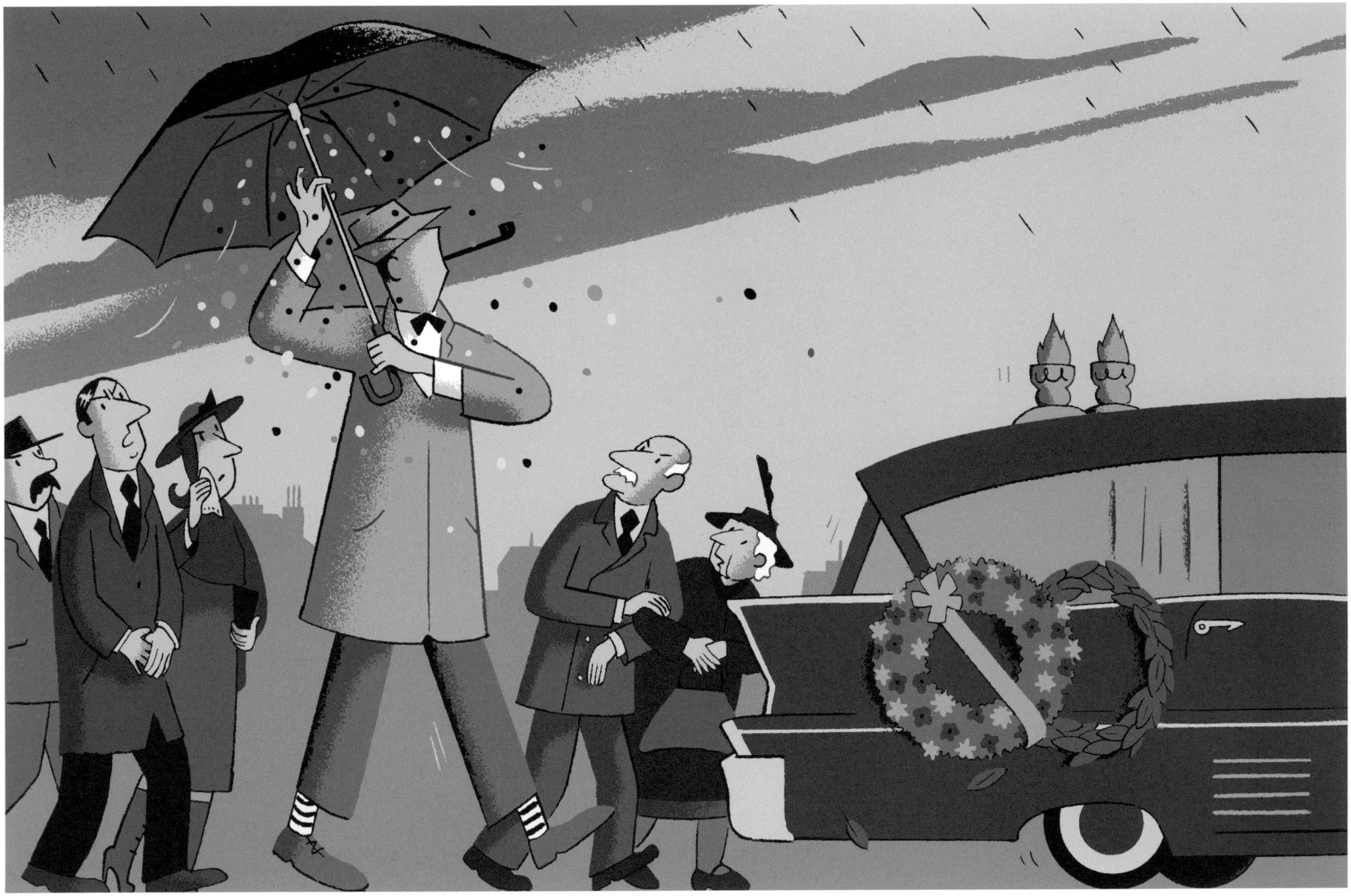

THE CROSSING

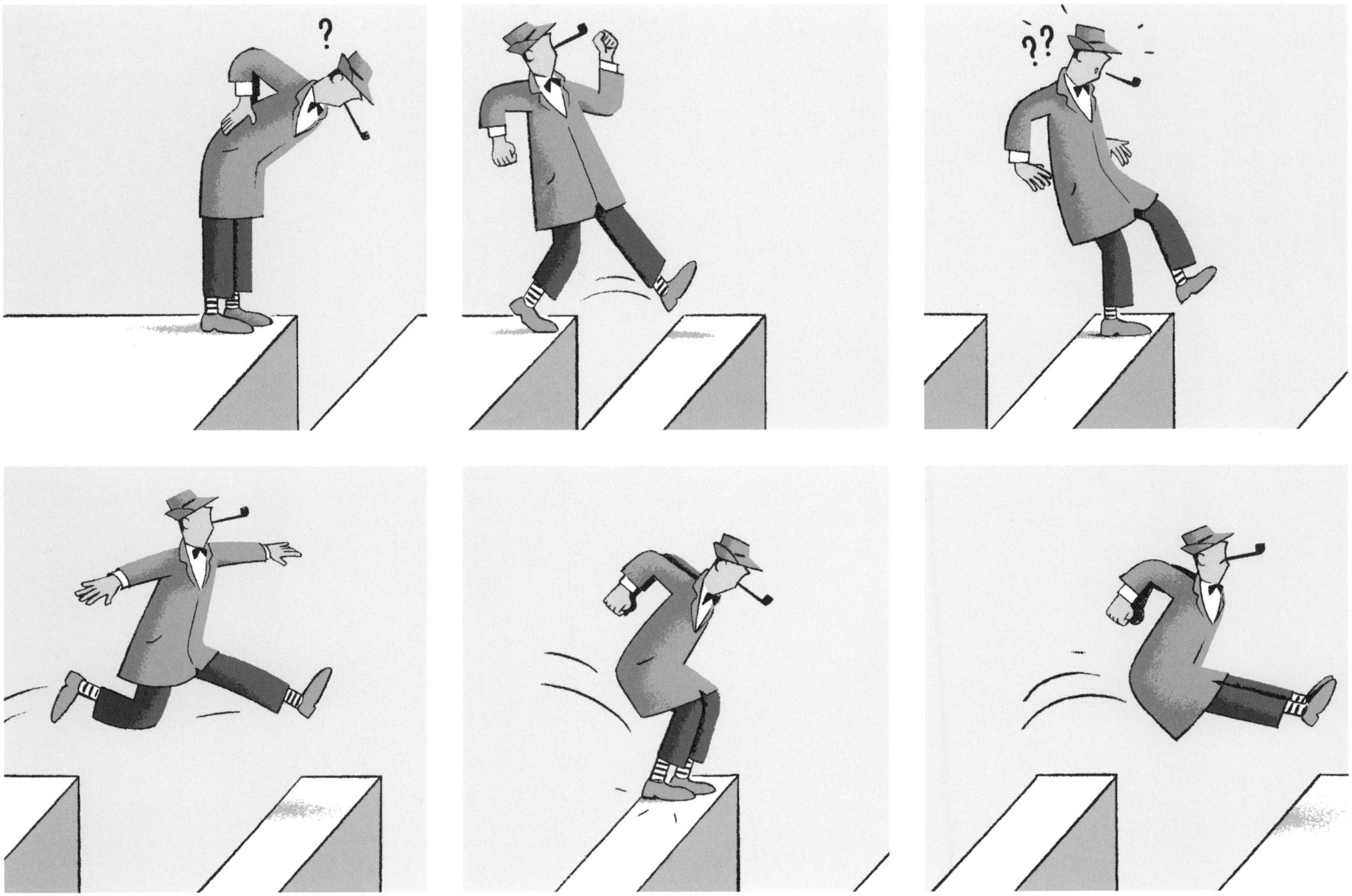
?
??

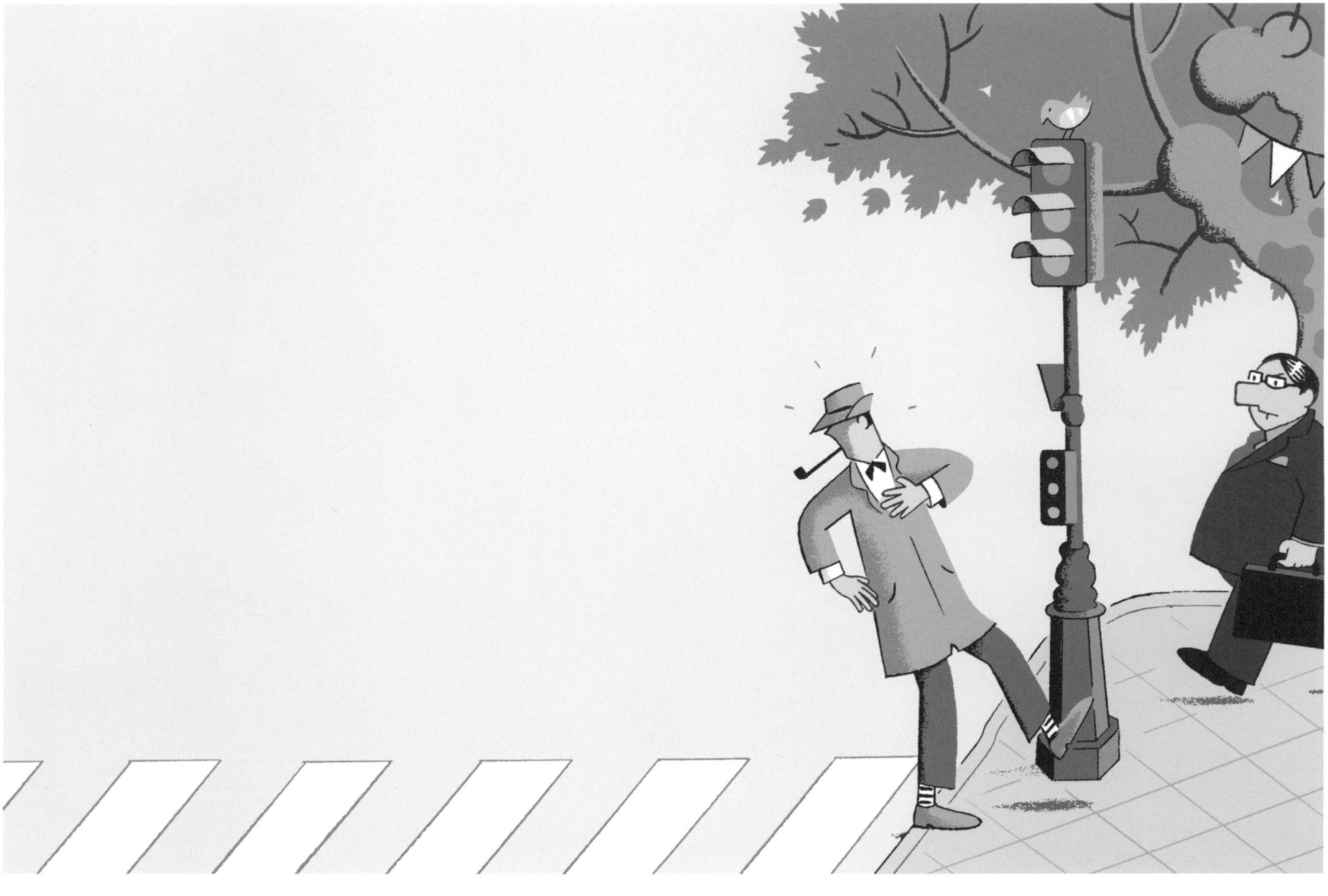

ATTENTION!

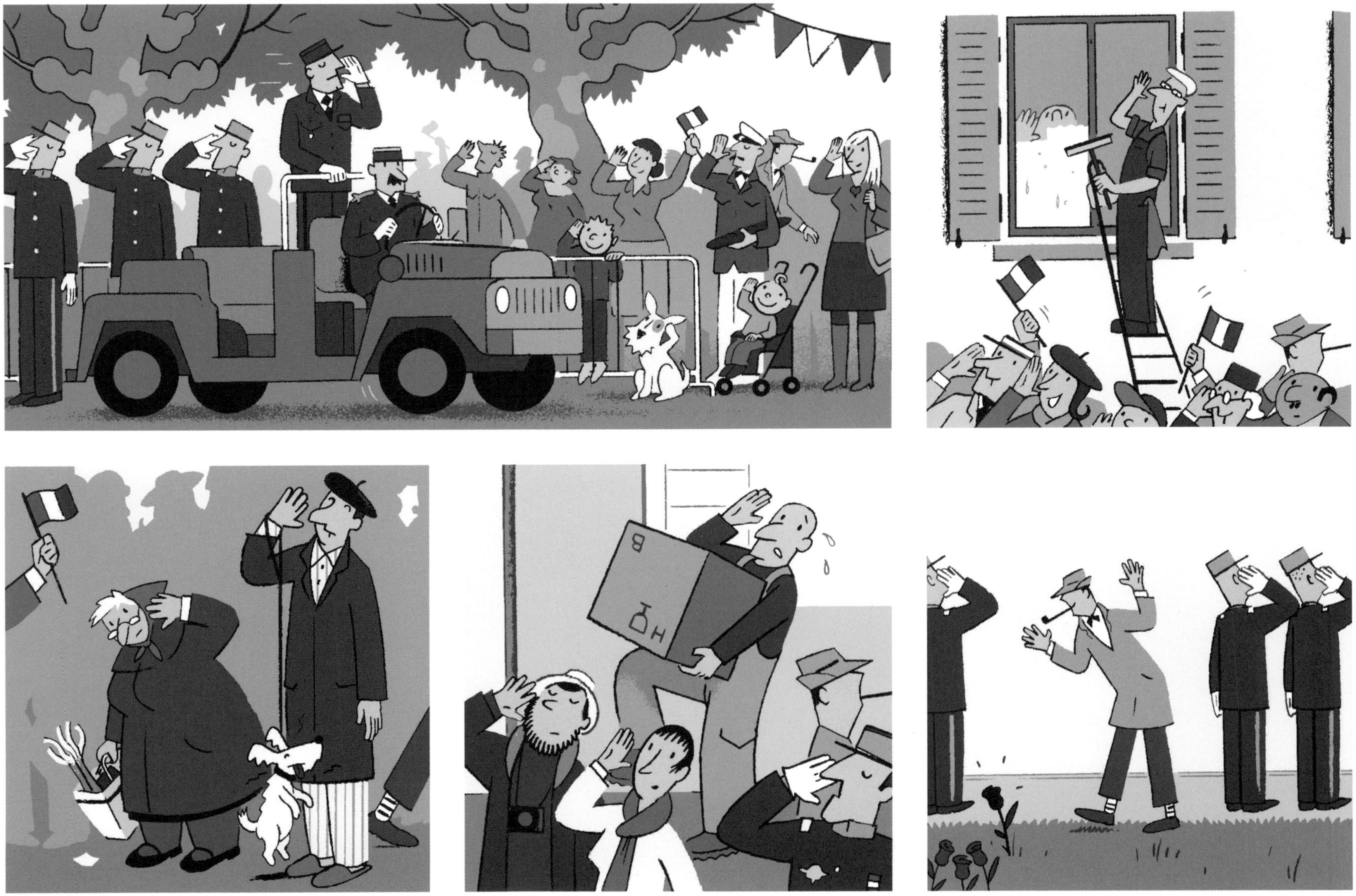

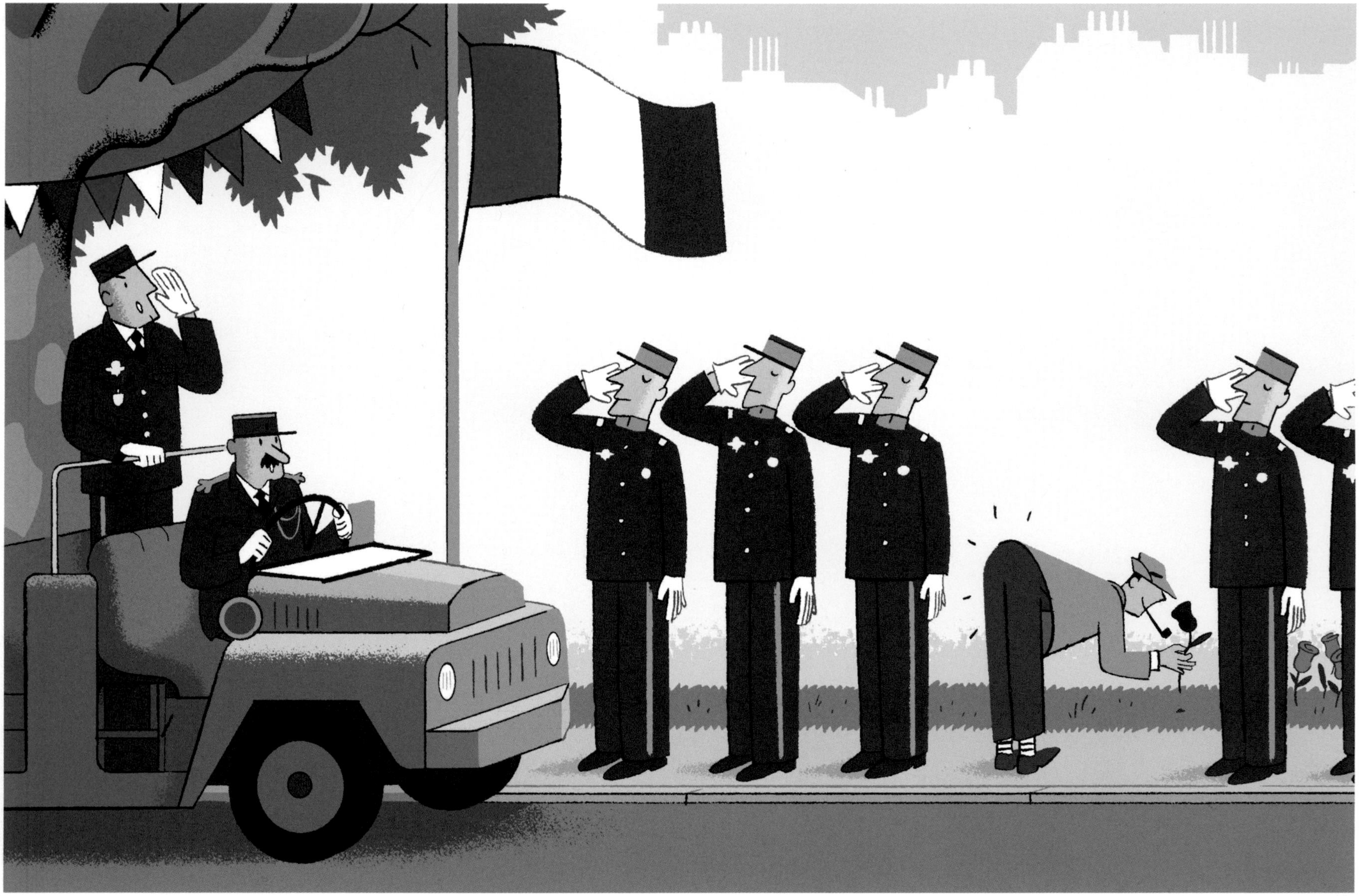

VALENTINE'S DAY

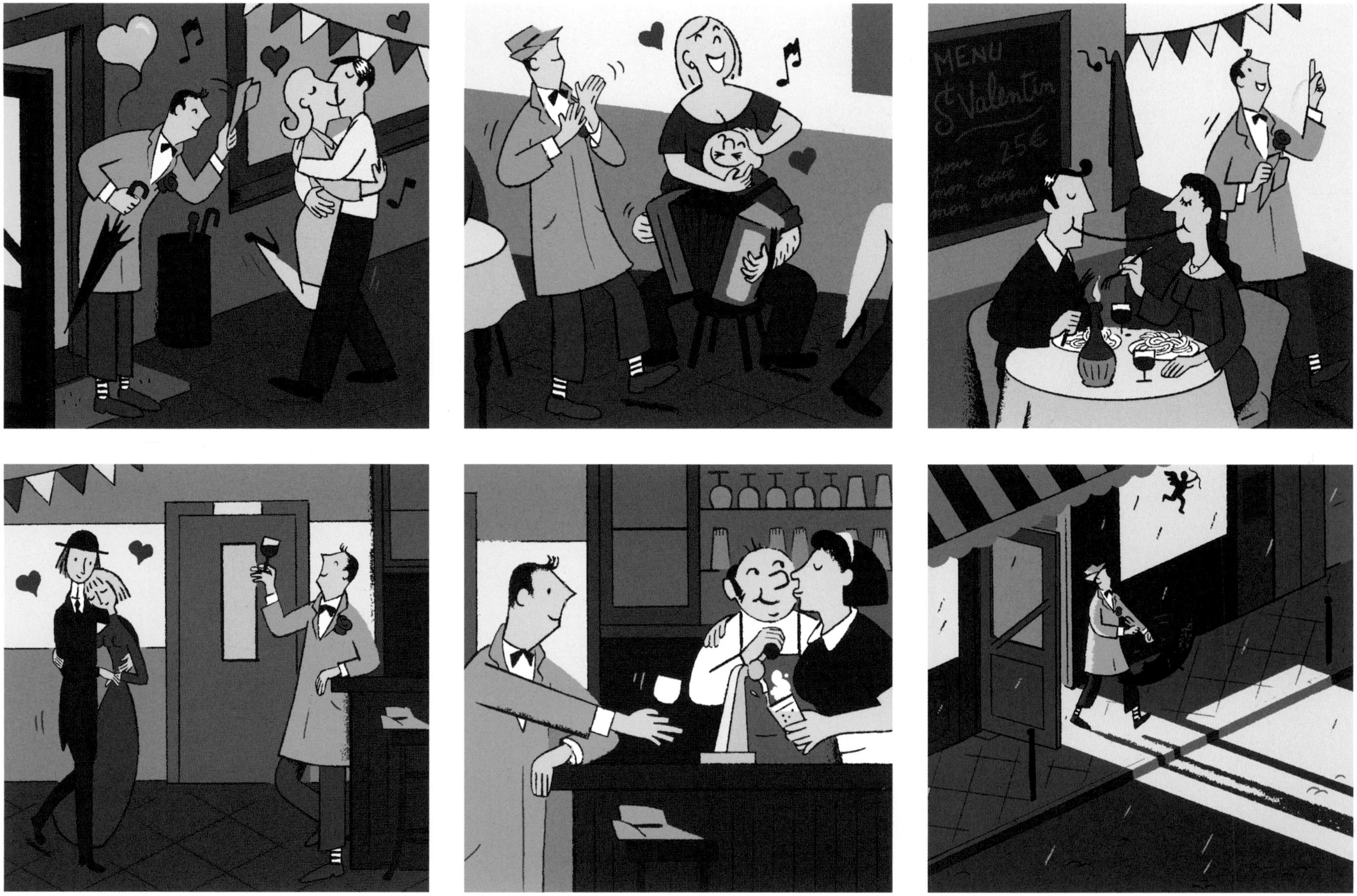
MENU
St Valentin
25€

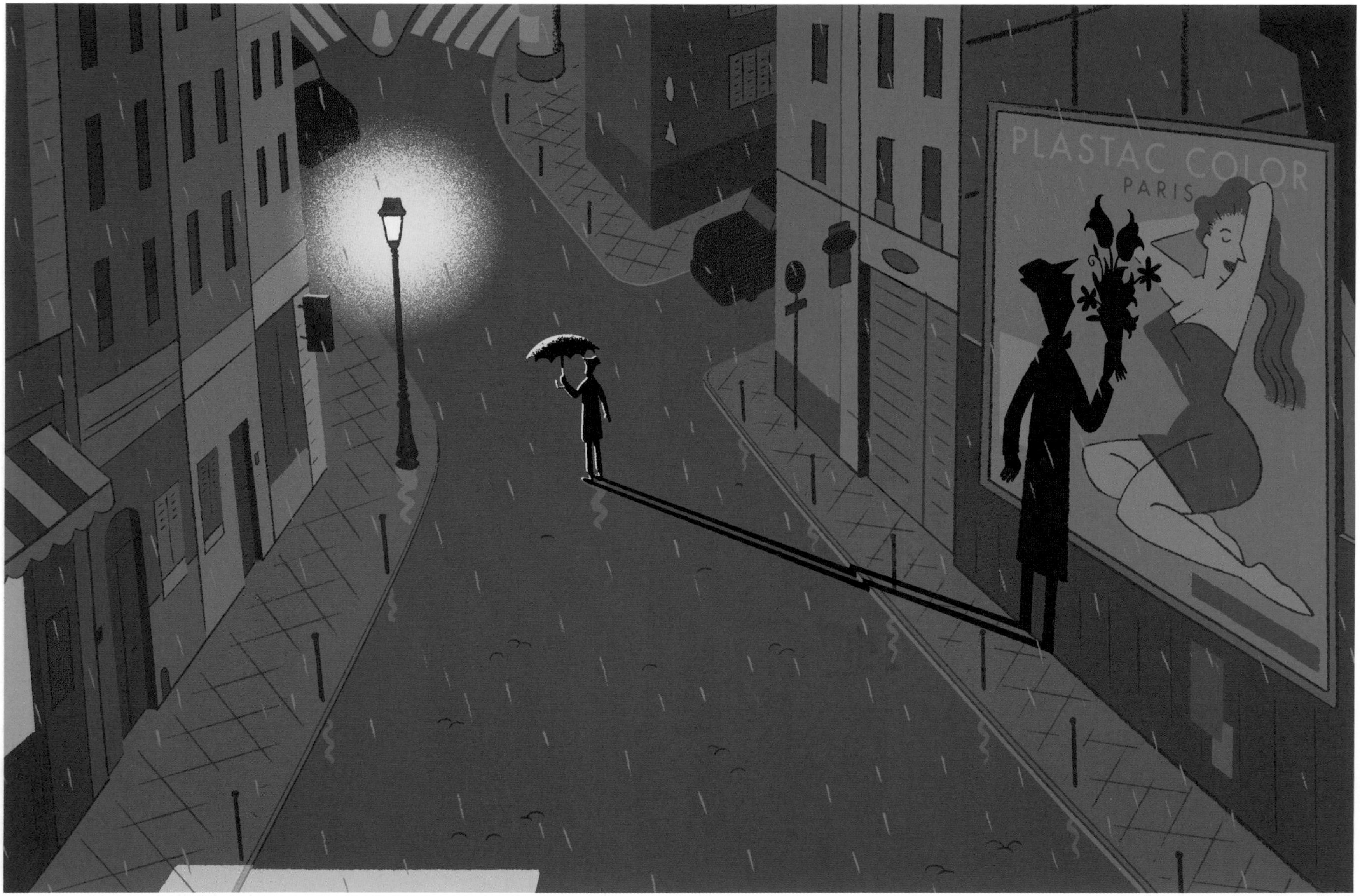
PLASTAC COLOR
PARIS

A TALL TALE

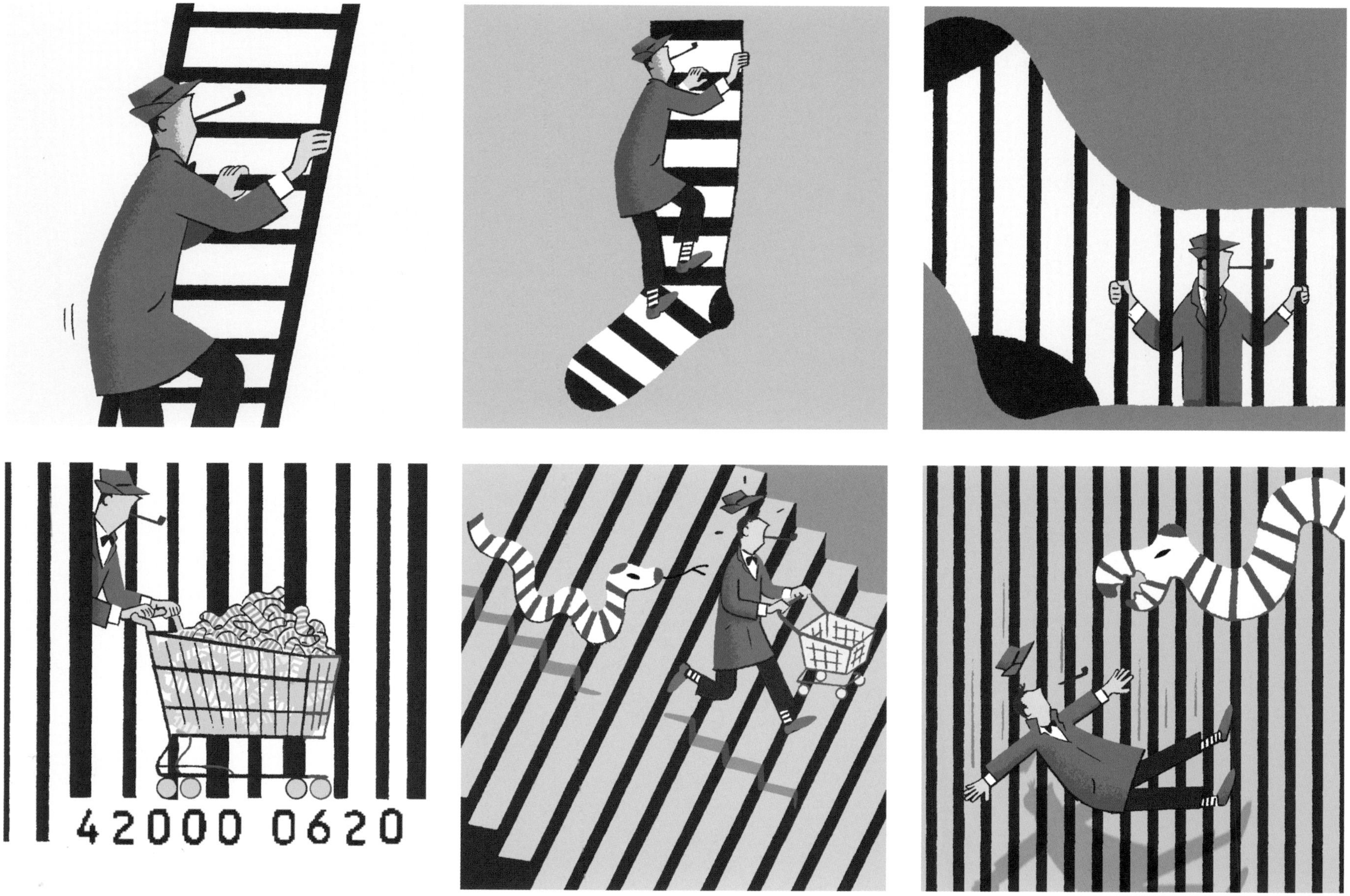
42000 0620

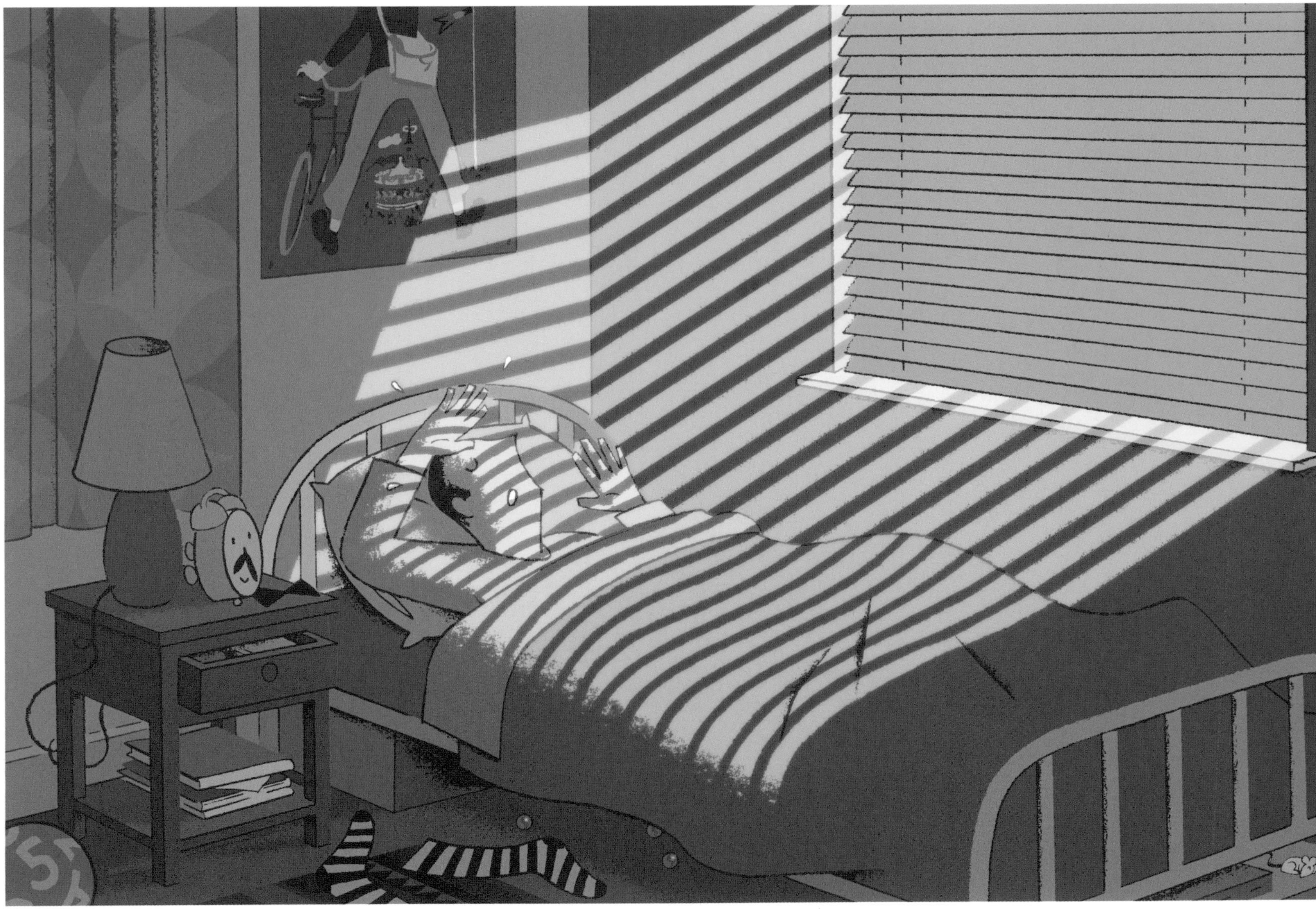

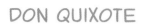

DON QUIXOTE

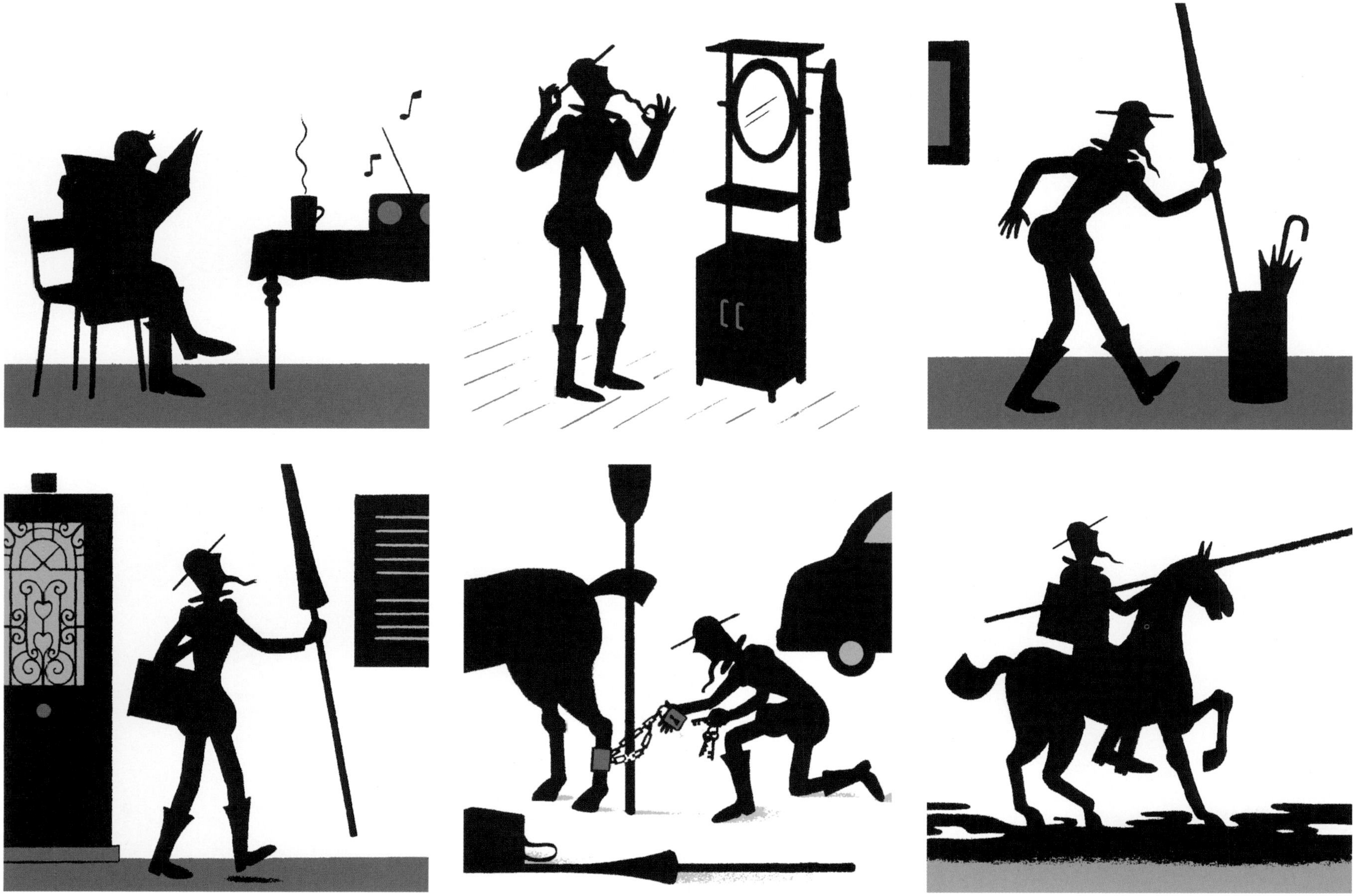

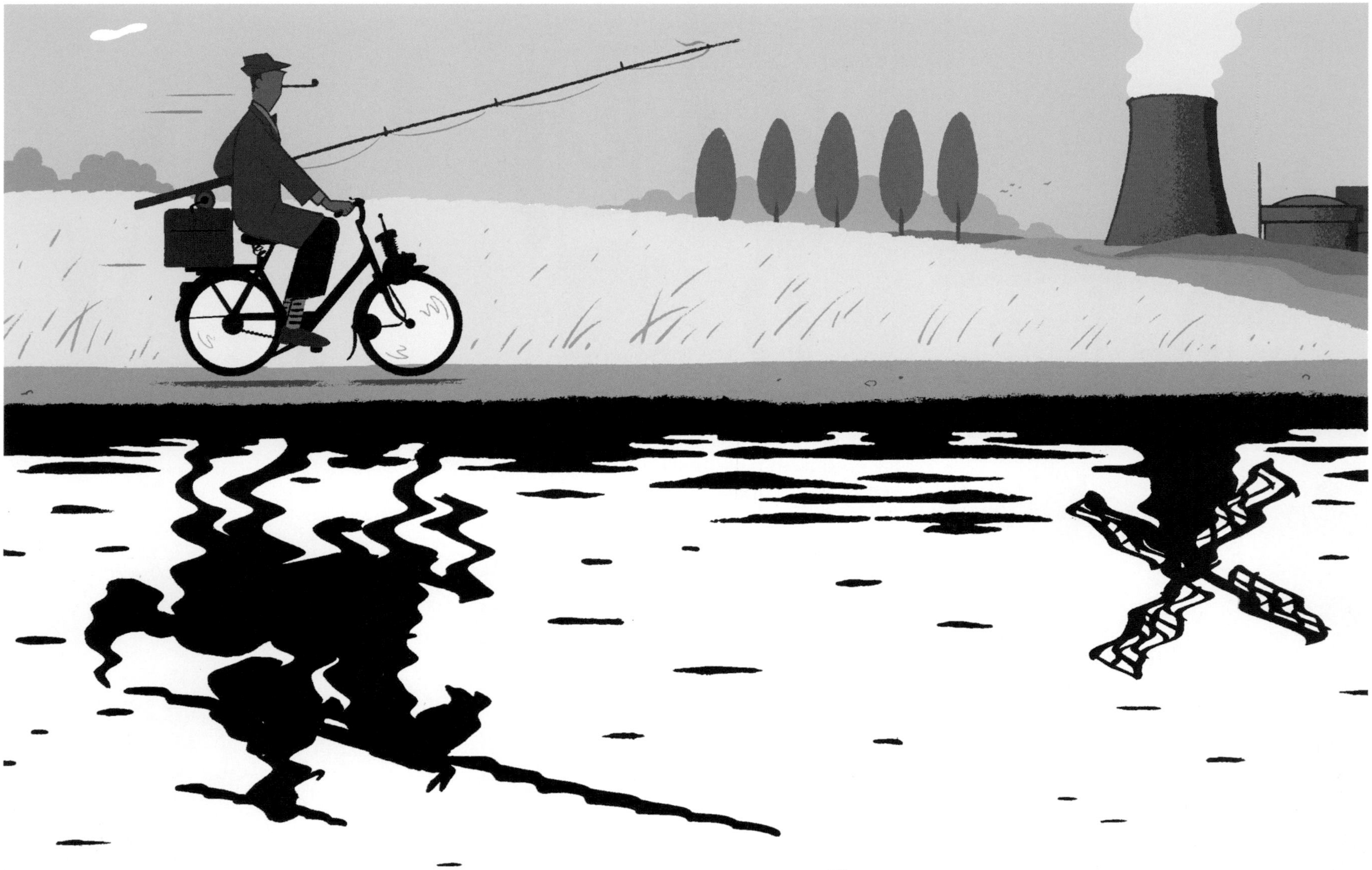

WATCH OUT, HULOT!

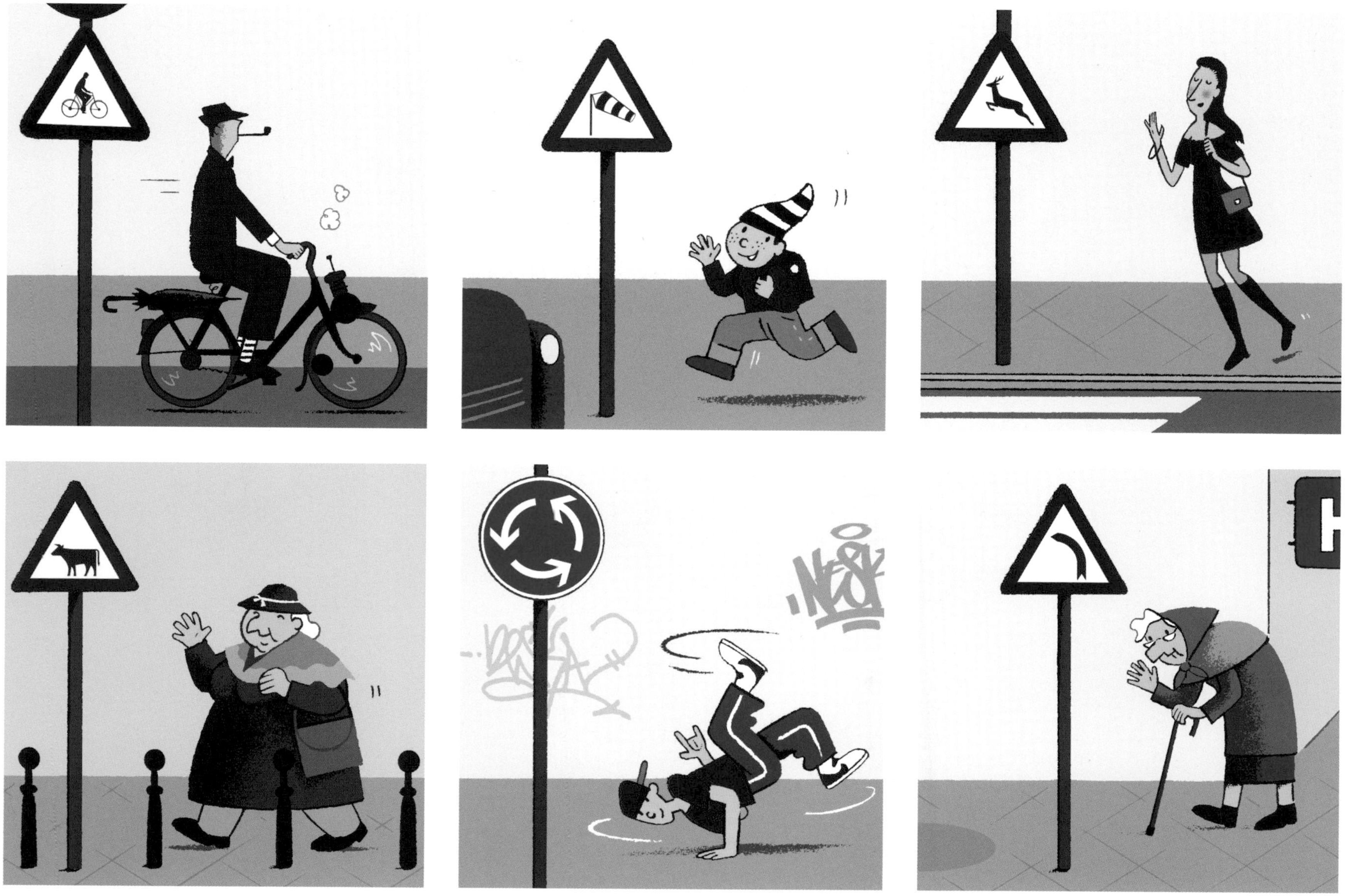

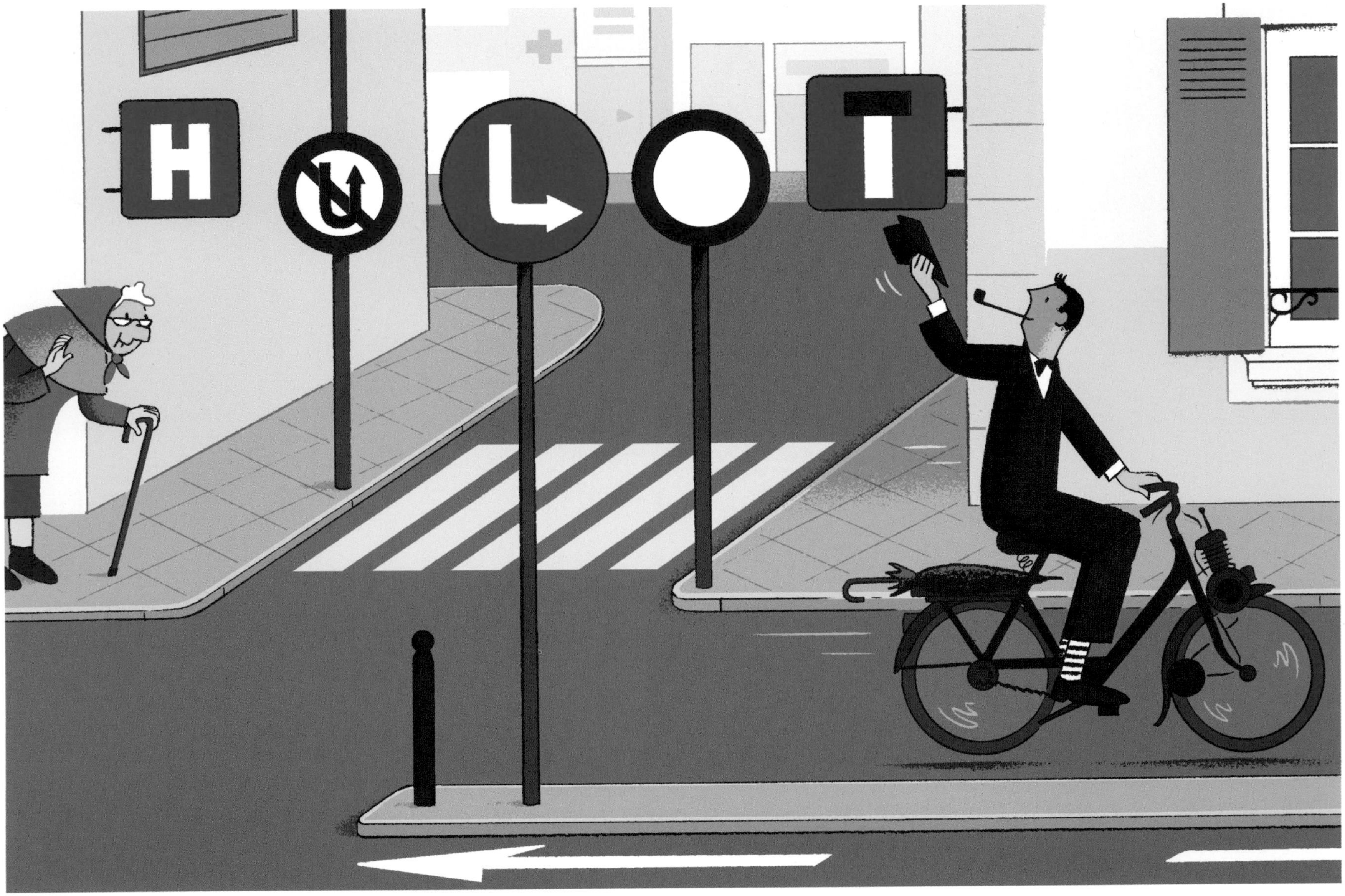
H
L
T

A BUTTERFLY MOMENT

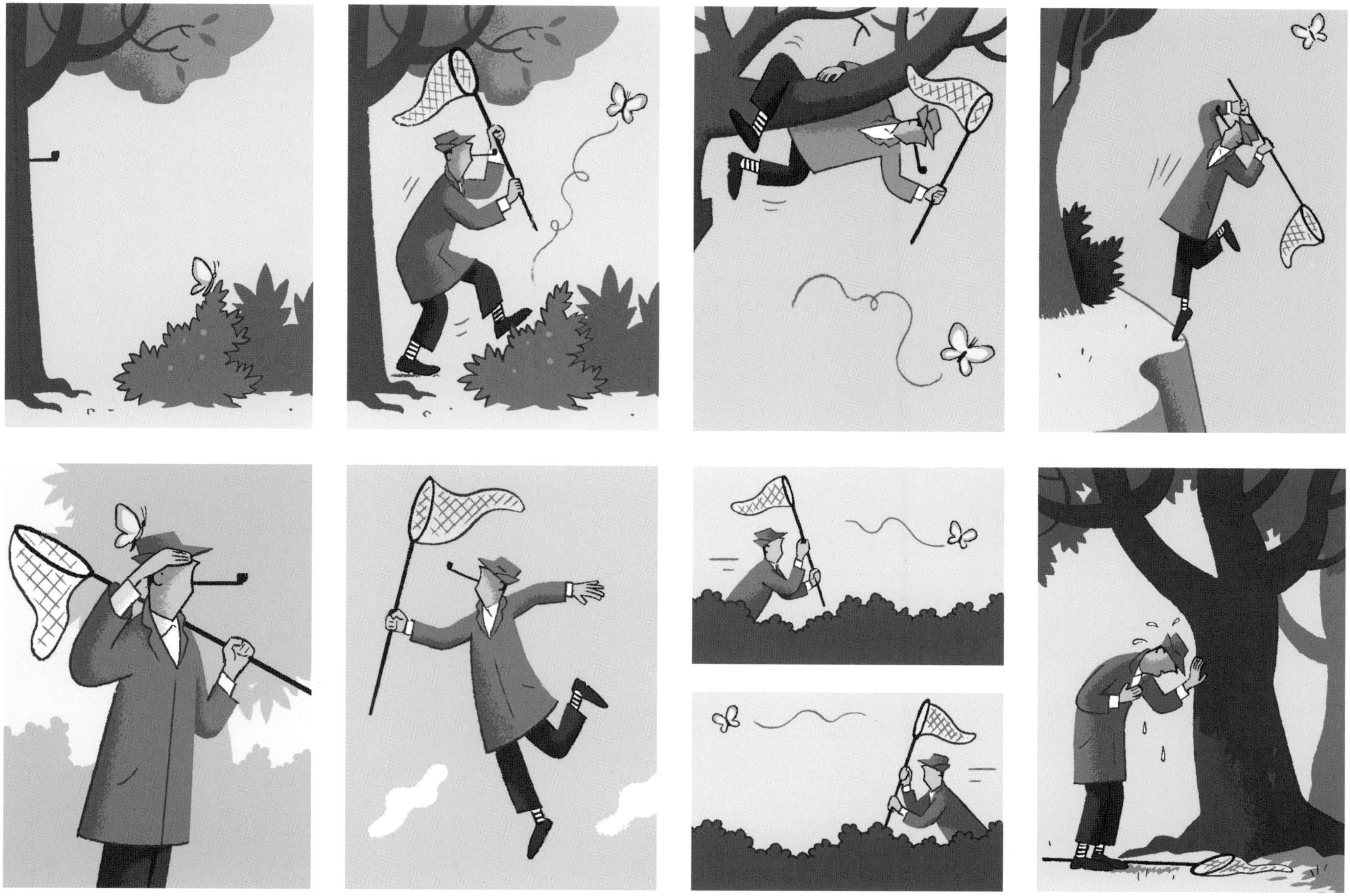

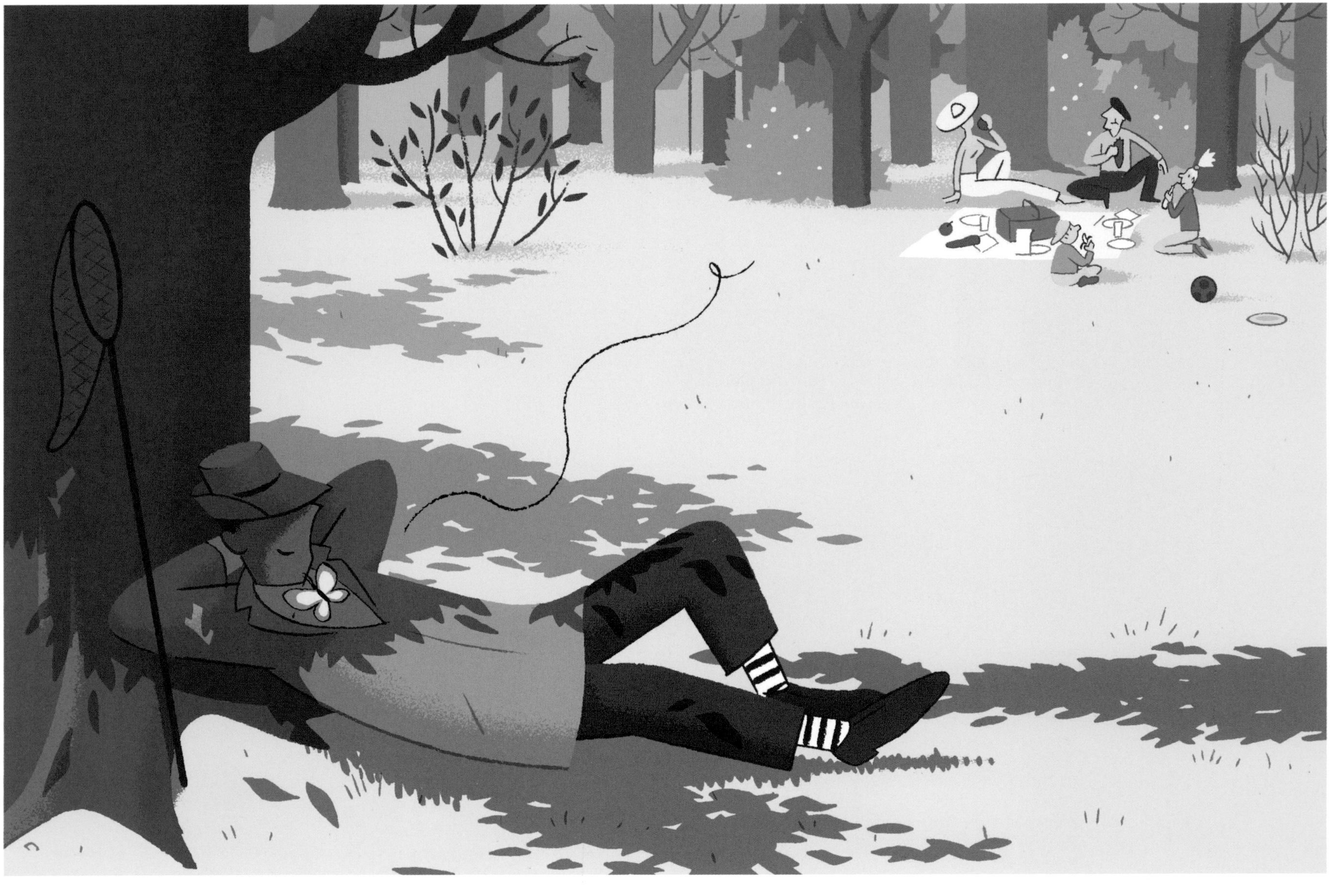

FRANÇOIS THE POSTMAN

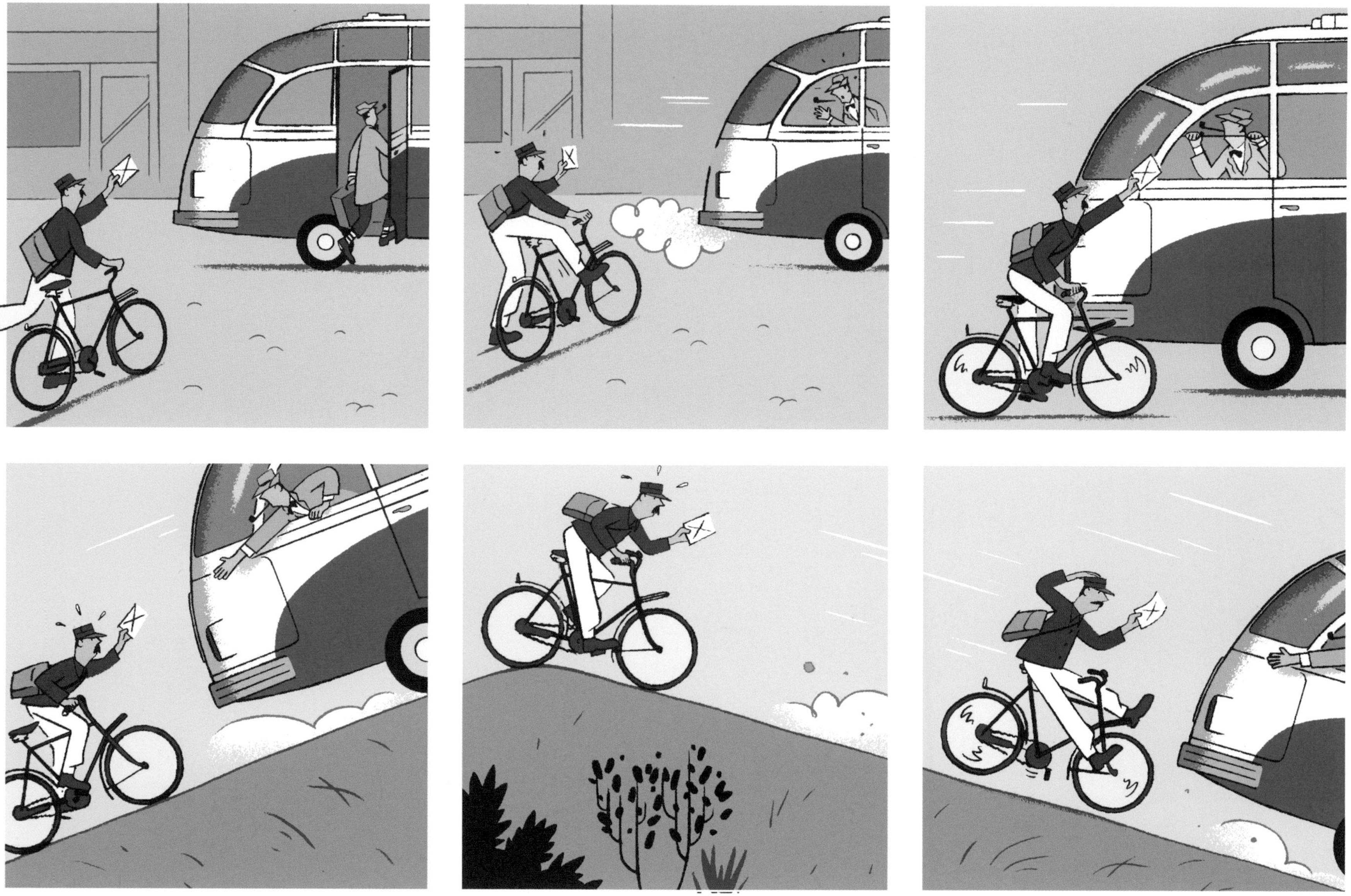

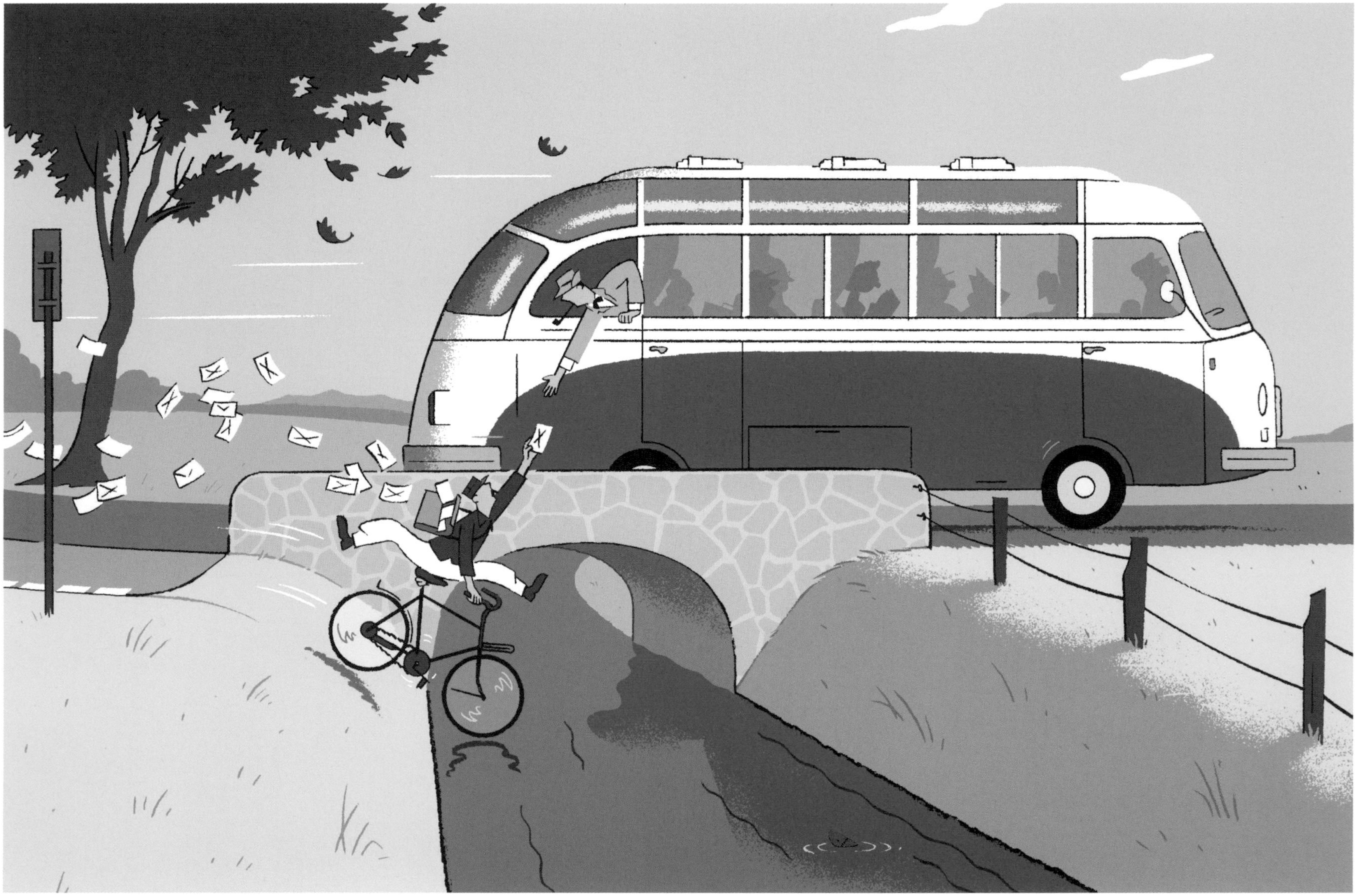

WANTED

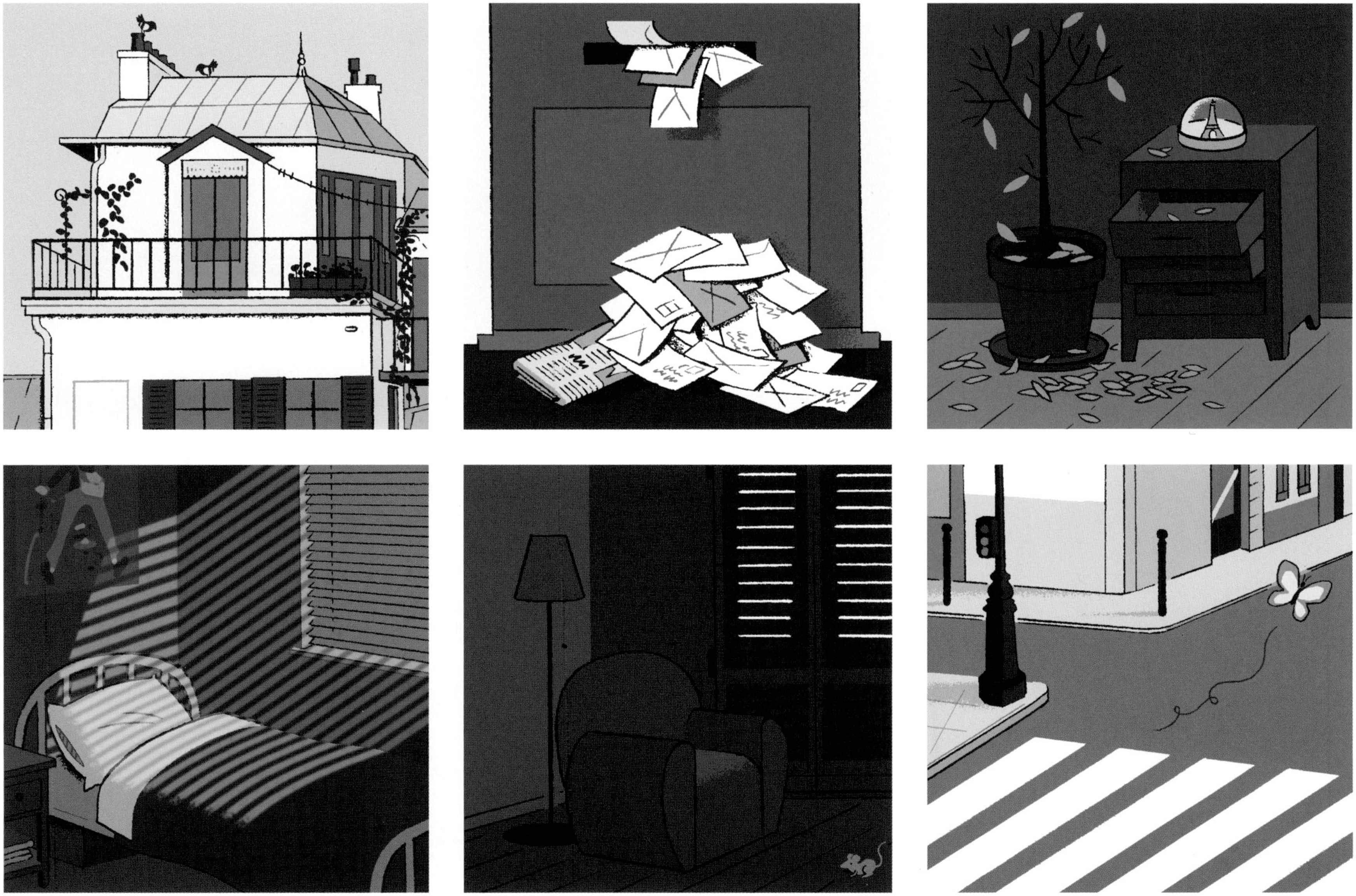

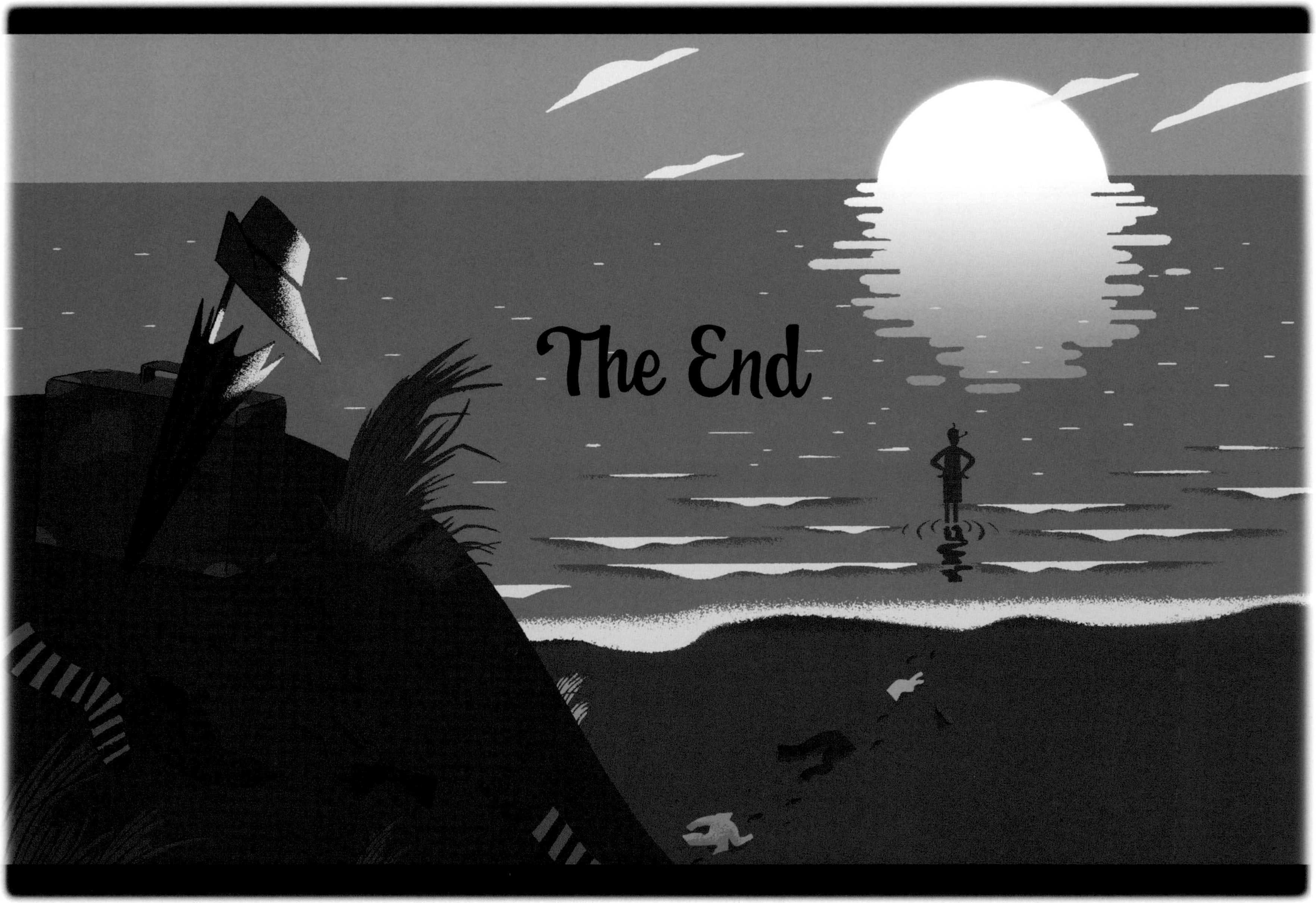
The End

JACQUES TATI'S LIFE AND WORK

Jacques Tati (originally named Jacques Tatischeff) was born in 1907 in Le Pecq, Yvelines, France. He became famous as a filmmaker, also working as a writer, comic actor, and director. Tati, originally working on the stage, celebrated his first success as an actor and director in 1949 with the film The Big Day (Jour de Fête). Monsieur Hulot, Tat''s most famous character, was already popular by the time he made his second film, Mr. Hulot's Holiday (Les Vacances de Monsieur Hulot) in 1953.

For his feature film My Uncle (Les Films de Mon Oncle, 1958), Tati won the Oscar for Best Foreign Language Film, in 1959. It was followed by PlayTime in 1967 and Traffic (Trafic) in 1971. Since the production of PlayTime was extremely expensive, however, the film was not very successful, and the financially troubled Tati slowly retreated away from the film business.

In 1977, Tati received an honorary Cesar from the French Film Institute for his lifetime contribution to cinema. Jacques Tati died in 1982 in Paris. His character, Monsieur Hulot, however, remains alive today.

MONSIEUR HULOT—
ANYTHING BUT RIDICULOUS

Monsieur Hulot, Jacques Tati's tragic-comic alter ego, was in a total of four movies dealing with a modernized world, in which he seems not to have the appropriate coping strategy. Technical achievements, the hectic pace, inhuman residential spaces, and a complex transportation system conspire to make his life difficult.

Hulot's blundering is emphasized by his distinctive dress—his wrinkled coat; his short trousers; his striped socks with straps; his hat, pipe, and umbrella—and make this lanky antihero all the more clumsy. Jacques Tati created the humble and naive Hulot, who must struggle against the cold and inhuman modern society.

DAVID MERVEILLE ON MONSIEUR HULOT

"It was in the year 2004 that I caught Hulot-fever. I hid a drawing of Monsieur Hulot in one my illustrations. The many responses I received about it proved that the attraction of this ingenious bumbling character is highly contagious. As a result, I honored Jacques Tati's films in two other children's books: Le Jacquot de Monsieur Hulot (2006) and Hello, Monsieur Hulot (2010).

"Translating Tati's films into the genre of the picture book seemed very logical to me: I could actually silhouette the behavior and gestures of Monsieur Hulot. It's ideal for a paper copy. The great film posters from Pierre Etaix demonstrated this.

"Also, Tati's access to film, his love for details, his keen powers of observation, his interest in things, his feelings about architecture, his economical use of dialogue, and his visual jokes have all encouraged me to develop Monsieur Hulot on paper. Hello, Mr. Hulot is being published in English by NorthSouth Books. Long live Hulot-fever!"